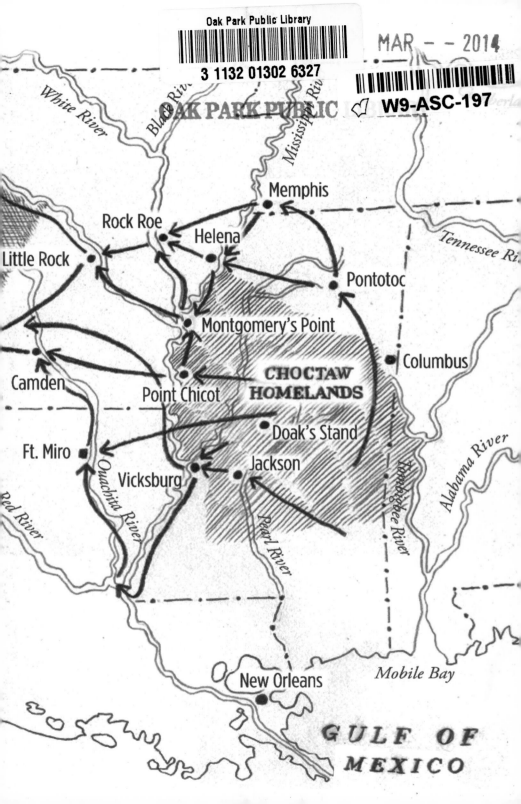

White River

Black River

Mississippi River

Tennessee River

Memphis

Rock Roe

Helena

Little Rock

Pontotoc

Montgomery's Point

Columbus

Camden

Point Chicot

CHOCTAW
HOMELANDS

Doak's Stand

Ft. Miro

Jackson

Ouachita River

Vicksburg

Alabama River

Tombigbee River

Red River

Pearl River

Mobile Bay

New Orleans

GULF OF
MEXICO

How I Became a Ghost

A Choctaw
Trail of Tears Story

The How I Became A Ghost Series
Book 1

Tim Tingle

THE ROADRUNNER PRESS
OKLAHOMA CITY

Published by The RoadRunner Press
Oklahoma City, Oklahoma
www.TheRoadRunnerPress.com

First Edition July 2013
Printed in January 2014 in the United States of America
by Maple Press, York, Pennsylvania
This book is available for special promotions, premiums, and group sales.
For details e-mail Director of Special Sales at info@theroadrunnerpress.com.

Publisher's Cataloging-In-Publication Data
(Prepared by The Donohue Group, Inc.)
Tingle, Tim.
  How I became a ghost : a Choctaw Trail of Tears story / Tim Tingle. — 1st ed.

  p. : ill., map ; cm. — (The how I became a ghost series ; bk. 1)

  Summary: A Choctaw boy tells the story of his tribe's removal from the only
land its people had ever known, and how their journey to Oklahoma led him to
become a ghost—one with the ability to help those he left behind.
  Interest age level: 009-012.
  Issued also as an ebook and an audiobook.
  ISBN: 978-1-937054-53-3 (hardcover)
  ISBN: 978-1-937054-55-7 (trade paper)
  ISBN: 978-1-937054-54-0 (ebook)
  ISBN: 978-1-937054-56-4 (audiobook)

  1. Choctaw Indians—Relocation—Juvenile fiction. 2. Indian Removal, 1813-
1903—Juvenile fiction. 3. Ghosts—Juvenile fiction. 4. Choctaw Nation of
Oklahoma—Juvenile fiction. 5. Choctaw Indians—Fiction. 6. Ghosts—Fiction.
7. Historical fiction. I. Title.

PZ7.T489 Ho 2013   [Fic]   2013935579

10 9 8 7 6 5 4 3 2

To my mentor Charley Jones,
who taught me the power of humor
in the Choctaw story

How I Became a Ghost

A Choctaw
Trail of Tears Story

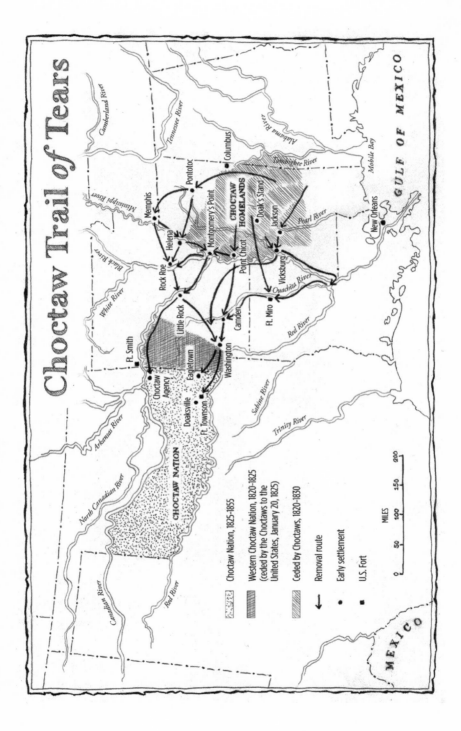

Choctaw Trail of Tears

GULF OF MEXICO

MEXICO

Cumberland River
Tennessee River
Mississippi River
Black River
White River
Arkansas River
North Canadian River
Canadian River
Red River
Sabine River
Trinity River
Red River
Ouachita River
Pearl River
Alabama River
Tombigbee River
Mobile Bay

New Orleans

Columbus
Pontotoc
Memphis
Helena
Rock Roe
Montgomery's Point
Point Chicot
Doak's Stand
Jackson
Vicksburg
Ft. Miro
Camden
Little Rock
Washington
Ft. Smith
Choctaw Agency
Eagletown
Doaksville
Ft. Towson

CHOCTAW HOMELANDS

CHOCTAW NATION

MILES
0   50   100   150   200

Choctaw Nation, 1825-1855

Western Choctaw Nation, 1820-1825
(ceded by the Choctaws to the
United States, January 20, 1825)

Ceded by Choctaws, 1820-1830

→   Removal route

•   Early settlement

■   U.S. Fort

Chapter 1

Talking Ghost
Choctaw Nation, Mississippi, 1830

MAYBE YOU HAVE never read a book written by a ghost before. I am a ghost. I am not a ghost when this book begins, so you have to pay very close attention. I should tell you something else. I see things before they happen. You are probably thinking, "I wish I could see things before they happen."

Be careful what you wish for.

I'm ten years old and I'm not a ghost yet. My name is Isaac and I have a mother and a father and a big brother, Luke. I have a dog, too. His name is Jumper and he is my best friend. We go everywhere together. We swim in the river together; we chase chickens together.

"Make sure Jumper does not catch any chickens!" My mother always yelled this from the back porch.

"Why can't Jumper catch chickens?" I asked my father one evening, as we sat on the porch watching the stars.

"That's your mother's rule," he said.

"But *why?*"

"Because Jumper won't wait for the chickens to be cooked," he said. "He'll chew the chickens and choke on the bones and bloody feathers. Would you want to eat bloody feathers?"

"No," I said. "Good rule."

"Then make sure Jumper follows it."

"*Hoke*," I said, which means "okay" in Choctaw.

Jumper and I, we take long walks in the woods together, we tug weeds from the corn stalks together, and we spend the day and night together.

"No dogs in your bed!" This was another rule of my mother's, but Jumper was smart. He waited until my mother fell asleep, then he climbed under the covers with me. In the morning, when he heard my mother making noise in the kitchen, he jumped out of bed.

Maybe she knew Jumper broke the rule. Maybe she smiled and let him get away with it. She was a good mother and we had a happy life, mostly. I had too many chores and too little free time, but I knew if I could just wait till I grew up, I'd have all the free time I wanted.

Then came the day that changed everything. Without any warning, I saw the ghosts. I also saw things before they happened.

My father rose early that morning, long before sunrise.

He left the house while it was still dark. He carried his shotgun and his bag of shotgun shells, so I knew he was going hunting.

I finished my chores and started tossing mudballs against the barn wall. Jumper barked and chased the mudballs, but only for a little while.

"I'm bored," Jumper said. "Let's chase chickens!"

We were on our way to the chicken pen when I saw my father coming home from the woods. He was carrying only his shell bag and his shotgun, so I knew something was wrong.

Usually he returned with a wild turkey or sometimes a deer. He never returned from a hunting trip with nothing. He walked through the back door and I followed him. He didn't say a word to me, just held up his hand to let me know I should stay outside.

I listened through the door.

"We must move," my father told my mother.

"What do you mean 'we must move'?" my mother asked. "You better move! Go back to the woods and catch us something to eat!" She was laughing.

"No," said my father, and he was not laughing. "There is Treaty Talk in town. We must move."

I was only ten, but I knew what Treaty Talk meant. It meant the *Nahullos* wanted something. *Nahullos* were people that lived a few miles away. They were not Choctaws, like us. We were nice to them and they were nice to us. But Treaty Talk always meant something else, and that something else was never nice.

3

My father took my mother by the hand and she gave him a strange look. He led her to their room, closing the door behind them. I was afraid of Treaty Talk and I didn't want to listen, not anymore.

Maybe it will all go away, I thought. You never know when your life is about to change. Treaty Talk is why I became a ghost.

Chapter 2

Treaty Talk

THE SUN ROSE HIGH in the sky, and I knew mother would have lunch ready soon. I was wrong. Everything about this day was wrong.

My father and mother kept talking, and I even thought I heard my mother crying. I waited on the front porch till Luke came home for lunch. He was twelve years old and never helped around the house. I had to do everything.

Hoke, sometimes he helped, but never enough.

"What's going on?" Luke asked.

"Mom and Dad are talking. Dad said there is Treaty Talk."

"Oh no," said Luke. "That means lunch will be late today. I'm not waiting around." He left to play stickball with his friends. *See what I mean?*

I circled the house and sat beneath the window of my parents' room, so I could hear what they were saying. My mother was crying, and she never cried.

"We have to be ready to go," my father said.

"Where will we go?" my mother asked.

"A long way from here. The Treaty has already been signed. We have till spring. But we should get ready to move."

We had no lunch that day. I fell asleep on the porch and Jumper rolled into a ball against my belly. When my mother finally stepped outside, the sun was peeking over the pine trees, ready for the moon to take over.

"Come with me," she said, taking my hand. Jumper trotted beside us.

"Where are we going?" I asked.

My mother said nothing. We walked through our garden of tomatoes and winding bean vines. We crossed the cornfield, where all the stalks were brown and dying. The evening air was already crispy cold and winter was coming. As we entered the woods, we met Luke walking from the river. He seemed upset.

"Luke, take Jumper home," my mother said. "Tell your father we will be home soon."

Luke nodded without saying a word.

He already knows what this is about, I thought.

We stepped from the woods and came upon a gathering of twenty old Choctaw men, scattered up and down the riverbank. I knew these men. They were the oldest men in town and they were our friends. We had supper at their homes and we knew their families.

One of the old men was Mister Jonah. He lived with his wife not far from us. As we watched, Mister Jonah took off his shirt and rubbed his back against a tree trunk. The tree was old, older than he was, and the bark was sharp and cracked.

Mister Jonah moved up and down, rubbing his back against the tree bark. His skin was dry and wrinkled. The bark cut into his skin and he started bleeding. Blood dripped from his back and covered the ground at his feet. His face was still as a stone, as if he didn't feel the pain, but I knew it had to hurt!

"Mother," I asked, "what is he doing?"

"Shhh," my mother whispered. "Don't talk. Just watch."

Soon all of the old men started rubbing their backs against the trees. When their backs were ripped open and bleeding, they sat in a puddle of their own blood. One man patted dirt on a friend's back to stop the bleeding. But the bleeding never stopped.

Hoke. *I should tell you this. Do not be afraid. This is how things are. When you will soon be a ghost, sometimes you see people before they are ghosts. You see how they will die. I didn't know it yet, but whenever I felt a warm shiver, I was about to see something no one else could see.*

I felt the warm shiver. I closed my eyes. When I opened them, Mister Jonah was sitting by the tree.

Suddenly, his hair burst into flames! He screamed and

waved his arms. He fell rolling to the ground. His arms were skinny logs and flames shot from his fingers.

No one moved to put the fire out.

I tried to run to him, but my mother held me tight. I jerked my arm free, took two steps, and stopped.

Mister Jonah sat with his back against the tree. His back was bleeding, like before, but his white hair fell over his shoulders. No burns on his arms. No burns anywhere.

The flames were gone. I looked at my mother. I was the only one to see the flames. They were flames for another day, a day that soon would come. If I was already a ghost, I might expect to see something like this. But I was not a ghost. Not yet.

"Mother, please tell me what is happening," I said.

"These men are saying good-bye to their home."

"They live in town. Their homes are in town."

My mother gripped my hand tight. "Come on," she said. "There is more to see."

Chapter 3

Dancing on the Stones

MY MOTHER LED ME to another spot on the river, where old Choctaw women were sitting on a pier. Some were the wives of the old men and some were widows.

I knew this pier. It was a long wooden pier with shallow water all around it. I fished from this pier, but very carefully, for the bottom of the river was covered with sharp stones. When I was only six, I went fishing by myself with my new cane fishing pole. I walked to the end of the pier and flung my line into the river. My cane pole slipped from my hand and I jumped in after it.

When I hit the river bottom I exploded in pain. The stones cut deep into the soles of my feet. I started jumping up and down, a stupid move, as every step I took meant more cuts.

I swam to the shore, leaving a bloody trail in the water behind me. I lost my first fishing pole that day and limped home in pain.

Yes, I knew this pier. While my mother and I watched, the old women sat on the edge of the pier, with their feet hanging over the water. Ten women sat on one side of the pier and ten sat on the other side. Four of the oldest women sat on the very end of the pier.

"They better be careful," I said.

"They know what they are doing," said my mother.

The sun peeked over the hills for one last look. Night was near. I leaned against my mother. The women started singing an old Choctaw song, rocking back and forth to the rhythm of the song. My mother joined them, singing in a whispery voice.

When the song was over, one woman shouted, "To the water!"

All at the same time, the old women jumped from the pier to the water. The stones must have cut their feet, but the women didn't seem to notice. They lifted their feet up and down and turned in circles in the water.

I could not believe what I was seeing. I gripped my mother's hand and looked up at her. Blood rose from the bottom of the river, and still the women danced. Their faces were the strangest thing of all.

The water was blood red, but the women showed no pain. They didn't squeeze their faces tight, like people do when they step on a sharp stone or stub their toe against a rock. The old women stared ahead like they were blind, like they saw nothing and felt nothing.

Missus Jonah was there. Her hair didn't turn to fire, like her husband's, not at first. I watched her dance with the others, till I felt the warm shiver again and closed my eyes.

"No," I whispered to myself. I shook my head. I didn't want to open my eyes, but I did.

Missus Jonah stopped dancing. The flames started at her feet, under the water. She screamed and tried to stomp out the flames. The fire climbed above the water and soon she was covered in flames.

The other women kept dancing on the stones. No one moved to help her.

Suddenly, just like before, the flames were gone. A few women limped to the shore. I looked to my mother. I knew she didn't see the flames.

As we left the pier, I looked over my shoulder at these tired old Choctaw women. Some were still dancing in the water.

"Mother, please tell me what is happening," I said.

"These old women are saying good-bye to their home," she said. "There is one more thing I want you to see. Then we can go. I will cook a good supper for you tonight."

We followed the river around a curve. The hills were lower here and the sun snuck through the trees. We came to my favorite swimming spot, where the river bottom was soft sand. A weeping willow tree hung over the water. My father once told me this tree was more than a hundred years old.

"It is the oldest willow in Choctaw country," he said.

11

The branches of the tree were long and thin and the leaves were light green. They hung over the river, like lime green walls of a small room.

In the center of this river room sat a Choctaw woman and her husband. They were the two oldest people in our town. Old Man and Old Woman, that is what we called them. They were both almost a hundred years old, and people spoke to them with respect.

My mother and I stood in the shadows and watched.

They sat in the shallow water, facing each other. Old Man dipped his hands in the river and lifted a double handful of wet, dripping sand. He smiled at his wife. She laughed and shook her head.

"No," she said, but she was smiling, too. He nodded his head up and down, then clapped his sandy hands to her face!

"Oh!" she squealed. She laughed and wiped the sand from her face. Then she scooped up two handfuls of sand and smacked him. These two old people acted like children. They laughed and played. They sat in the river and splashed and threw sand all over each other.

I knew what would happen next. The warm shiver came and I closed my eyes. After what I had already seen, I was afraid to look. I didn't want to see Old Man and Old Woman covered in flames.

What I saw was even worse.

When I opened my eyes, Old Man was covered in sores. His face was swollen and his eyes were closed. He shook as if he were freezing to death.

He turned to me, begging me to help him.

Old Woman had ugly yellow sores on her neck and face. She fell into the river and bubbles floated from her nose. She kicked and trembled, rolling her head from side to side.

Old Woman looked at me and tried to speak. A stream of bubbles rose from her lips. Then she stopped moving.

I closed my eyes again. When I looked up, everything was like before. Old Man and Old Woman were laughing and playing, like children in the river.

I did not have to look at my mother. I knew she hadn't seen the sores on Old Man and Old Woman. On our way home, I asked her again, "Mother, what were the old people doing?"

"They are saying good-bye to their home," she said.

"Their homes are in town."

"No," said my mother. "Their houses are in town. This river, this dirt, this is their home. This is our home. Your father was right. There is Treaty Talk and we must move. It is time to say good-bye to our home."

Chapter 4

Fire in the Hair

WE RETURNED FROM the river. While Luke and Jumper and I played in the backyard, Mother cooked supper. Everybody was quiet while we ate. No one said anything about the old men and women at the river. No one said anything about Treaty Talk, but the silence spoke louder than words. Soon after supper we went to bed.

It happened after midnight.

I felt no shiver. This was real.

I smelled smoke and jumped out of bed. The room was dark, but I could smell the smoke. It was behind me so I turned around. The smoke was still behind me. I turned around again. The smoke was still behind me. I turned around and around. I was scared now.

Why couldn't I see the smoke? I wanted to scream.

I felt the skin of my neck burning. My long hair was in flames! I heard a loud *crack* and fire fell from the ceiling. I grabbed my blanket and wrapped it around my shoulders, smothering the flames.

When I opened the door, a cloud of fire hit me in the face. I ran through the flames and out the front door. My mother and father and Luke stood in the yard. Jumper was there, too. He leapt in my arms.

"We thought you ran out back," my mother said. "We called for you. The smoke was so thick."

The roof of our house was burning. Bright specks of fire floated in the night sky.

"Run next door and wake the neighbors!" my father said. "They can help us put the fire out."

Luke and I ran to the neighbor's house, but it was burning, too. We flung open the door and ran inside. Everybody was still sleeping.

"Wake up!" Luke shouted. With squeals and screams our neighbors jumped out of bed and fled their burning house.

"Run to the church and ring the bell!" said my father. "Wake everybody up!"

Luke and I started for the church, but my father stopped us.

"Wait! Look there." He was pointing to the river. Men rode horses from the river, *Nahullo* men, and they carried burning torches. While we watched, they rode to the church. They leapt from their horses and threw the torches high, aiming for the house where the missionaries lived.

We stood in the street watching, my family and our neighbors. The torches made slow circles, turning over and over, followed by a trail of sparks. Like fiery comets, twenty flaming torches fell from the sky. They landed on the roof of the house and the dry cedar boards burst into flames.

The missionaries were visiting another Choctaw town that week, but the *Nahullos* didn't know that. They would have burned the house down with the missionaries inside asleep.

A *Nahullo* man ran into the church and climbed the ladder to the bell tower. He dropped his torch on the roof and soon the church was a swirling mass of flames.

What about the Bibles? I thought. *And the songbooks?*

The men shouted and pointed to us. One man took his shotgun from his horse and aimed it at my family. My father threw himself over us and we fell to the ground.

Pow! The noise from the shot was loud.

"Ohhhh," a neighbor shouted.

My face was covered in blood, the blood of our next-door neighbor. His shoulder was bleeding. My father took off his shirt and wrapped it around him.

"Run," my father said, "and stay together." We hurried to the deep woods at the end of town. The *Nahullo* men jumped on their horses and followed us.

When we entered the woods, my father pushed us into a clump of bushes. We knelt and huddled close together. My father whispered in my ear.

"Take a deep breath and do not move." I nodded and sucked in the cold night air. Jumper climbed under my shirt. My father put his hand behind my head and pushed my face to the ground. He did this to protect me.

I lay with my face on the wet ground. A man rode his horse into the woods. He was so close. I could have reached out and touched the hoof of his horse. Even Jumper knew to be quiet. I felt him warm against my belly.

"I don't see them!" the man yelled.

"Let them go," said another man. "They will wander around in the swamps till we find 'em. No place else for them to go. Their homes are burning."

"We should have done this a long time ago," he whispered to himself, but we were close enough to hear him.

We stayed in the bushes all night and watched the houses burn. The flames made a crackling sound and by morning every house had fallen to the ground.

I learned something about houses that night. This will sound strange. On the night I almost became a ghost, I learned something about houses.

Houses are alive.

Every house shook before it fell. Like Jumper shaking water after a swim, every house shook. Every house shouted, too. As loud as the thunder, every house also shouted. One by one, every house shouted and fell.

I lay on the ground with my father, my mother, my brother Luke, and Jumper. Our neighbors crouched on the ground nearby. We watched our houses shout and shake and fall.

"I wonder if anyone burned in their house," Luke said.

"The Jonahs," I told him. "Mister Jonah and Missus Jonah."

"How do you know that?" Luke asked.

I did not answer him.

My mother looked at me. Of course, she knew. She knew everything.

"There is nothing we can do," my father said.

"We can stay together," said my mother.

Chapter 5

Swamp Choctaws

"WE SHOULD GO NOW," my father said. "If we wait till morning they could find us."

We walked deeper into the woods, far away from town. We knew where we were going. For Choctaws, the safest place was the swamp. *Nahullos* never came to the swamp. We hunted there. We fished there. Whenever we wanted to be safe we always went to the swamp.

All night we walked the muddy ground. The trees were thick and covered with vines and thorny bushes grew everywhere. We arrived at the swamp as the sun was rising.

We were not alone. Every Choctaw from our town, those who were still alive, had come to the swamp. The old women were limping as they walked, and I remembered their dance on the stony river bottom.

The swamp water was green and sticky. I carried Jumper, and we crossed the swamp on logs and old wooden planks.

"Let me swim!" Jumper said.

"No," I told him. "The water is dirty green. You can't shake swamp water off."

By morning, a hundred Choctaws gathered on the island in the middle of the swamp. My father led us to a thick pine tree. Old Man and Old Woman from the sandy river bottom sat at the base of the tree. Old Man stood up and everybody hushed.

"We can talk about last night later. Now we go to work. Young men will get the meat. Deer and squirrels are all around us. The swamp is full of fish.

"Young women will look for wild onions and berries. Older men will build houses, lean-tos. Winter is coming. We will spend the day working and have our first meal tonight."

"What will the older women do?" a young man asked. Everyone grew very quiet. No one looked at him. They were too embarrassed. Old Man smiled.

"The older women do not need me to tell them what to do," he said.

When the gathering was over, my father spoke to Luke and me. "I'll build us a lean-to. You two see what you can catch for supper."

I was only ten years old, but I could catch a squirrel with a blowgun. Luke and I hollowed out two long stalks of river cane. Using a sharp stone for a knife, we carved darts from tree limbs and tied bird feathers to one end.

"I think we're ready," Luke said. "Let's see if they work. You go first."

I stuck a dart in my blowgun and lifted it to my mouth. Aiming at a skinny pine tree twenty feet away, I took a deep breath and blew. The dart stuck in the tree trunk!

"Good shot," Luke said.

"See how close you can get to my dart," I challenged him.

Luke got a serious look on his face. He loaded his dart, took his breath, and blew. The dart missed the tree, didn't even come close, but I didn't fall for it. I knew Luke was a better shot than that.

"You did that on purpose," I said. Luke laughed and slapped my shoulder.

"*Hoke*," he said. "You're a smart little brother, Isaac. Let's go hunting."

"I've been waiting for this," Jumper said.

Jumper dashed to a clump of trees on the far end of the swamp island. Luke and I hurried after him. Jumper circled a tall pine and jumped up and down, growling and scratching the tree trunk.

"Good boy, Jumper," said Luke. We heard a scattering of leaves and the chirping of squirrels.

By suppertime we had enough squirrels to feed the family.

While we were hunting, my father and his friends had built the lean-tos. They cut pine limbs, tied the limbs together with vines, and leaned them against the giant cypress trees. By nightfall, every Choctaw family had a home. Not real homes, not like before, but when it rained we could stay dry.

With blowguns we caught our food. With lean-tos we had a place to sleep. Young women found wild onions and leafy green vegetables, while the older women dug cooking holes. They covered the holes with green branches so the *Nahullos* couldn't see our cooking fires.

That is how we lived. A week later, winter came. Night and day we shivered from the cold wind and icy rainfall.

And every day I grew closer to being a ghost.

Chapter 6

Men with Blankets

WE WERE NOT AFRAID of the *Nahullos* in the swamp. *Nahullos* didn't know the swamp. Snakes and alligators lived in the swamp, and it was hard to tell the ground from a mudhole. We Choctaws knew to be careful, with every step, but the *Nahullos* didn't know the swamp.

But winter changed everything. The swamp froze in the winter. Snakes slept underground and even the deepest mudholes turned to ice. The *Nahullos* could ride their horses over the frozen swamp.

One morning I woke up and the world was white.

Even before I opened my eyes I felt the white. Everything was quiet, and I peeped through the branches of our lean-to. Ice hung from the trees and mounds of snow covered the ground.

This was a warning. On this white day, many people would become ghosts. Many of the old men and women would become ghosts, and many children, too.

"Be very quiet," my mother said. "*Nahullos* are coming." I looked for my father, but he was gone. I held Jumper close.

I heard the horses first. They snorted and wheezed, and soon I heard the wagons. The wooden wagon wheels crunched and cracked the ice. I was afraid. Everyone was afraid. My father came into the lean-to.

"Stay here," he said.

The wagons slowly crossed the swamp and came into our lean-to town. Everyone hid. We were so quiet. We looked through the branches.

The men on the wagons were *Nahullo* soldiers. They wore uniforms. They jumped to the ground and reached for something in the wagons.

"Guns," Luke said. "They will shoot us."

"Shhhh," my mother whispered.

When the men turned around, they didn't have guns. They had blankets and they smiled. We were all freezing from the cold and the *Nahullo* soldiers had blankets.

"The blankets are for you!" a soldier shouted.

At first no one moved.

"Come and get the blankets!" another soldier yelled.

Old Man was the first Choctaw to leave his lean-to. Old Woman followed after him. The soldier smiled and gave Old Man a blue blanket. Old Man wrapped himself in the blanket and turned around for everyone to see.

"Nice and warm. *Yakoke*," said Old Man.

Old Woman took the second blanket and threw it over her shoulders.

"*Yakoke*," she said. She buried her head in the blanket and shook with joy.

Many Choctaws ran for the blankets. Mothers and children took the blankets. Fathers took enough blankets for everyone in their lean-to.

"*Yakoke!*" they told the soldiers. "Thank you!"

When I tried to leave our lean-to, my mother grabbed my arm and pulled me back inside.

"Sit down," she told me.

"I want a blanket," I said.

My mother held my head on her shoulder. She ran her hand through my hair, and I felt warm next to her. "We do not need their blankets," she whispered in my ear.

Luke tried to run for a blanket, but my mother pulled him back, too. She drew him inside the lean-to.

"Sit next to me," she said.

Luke sat on one side of my mother and I sat on the other. My father stood over us and watched. No one left our lean-to that morning.

"We do not need their blankets." My mother whispered this. Over and over she whispered, "We do not need their blankets."

After the soldiers left, everyone was happy. For a few days, everyone was happy.

"We don't have to be afraid anymore," Old Man shouted.

25

"We can build our fires high!" said Old Woman.

Our neighbors left their lean-tos and visited and laughed. Jumper barked and played with the other dogs. But my father and mother were not happy, not like the others. We were still freezing cold.

"Luke and Isaac, stay in the lean-to," my father said. "Do not go near anybody. Stay here."

While everybody else slept that night, my father and Luke went hunting. They returned with two small squirrels, and we cooked them over the fire for breakfast.

Old Man saw the smoke from our cooking fire and stuck his head under our lean-to.

"Come outside," he said. "I'll share my blanket."

I looked at his face. I felt the warm shiver from inside, like before. I closed my eyes, and when I opened them, Old Man was not smiling. His face was red and swollen and a red sore lay next to his nose. Then another sore appeared, on his lip. Soon his cheeks were covered in sores.

Old Man fell to the ground. He rolled out of his blanket and buried his face in the snow.

"I don't want to see this!" I shouted. I covered my face with my hands.

"What is wrong with you?" Luke said. He pulled my hands apart. When I looked up, Old Man was staring at me. The sores were gone.

"Are you all right?" he asked.

"Yes," I said. "I am sorry. I am cold, that's all." I didn't want to lie, but I couldn't tell him what I knew. I knew that Old Man and Old Woman would soon be ghosts.

How I Became a Ghost

I almost became a ghost that day. If my mother hadn't pulled me back, I would have become a ghost.

How could my mother have known?

Years later, after I did become a ghost, I asked myself. *How did she know?*

Chapter 7

Snow Monsters

HOKE. *EVERYTHING WAS sad, rotten sad. I was ten years old. This was no way to live! In many ways, when you are ten years old, you are smarter than grown-ups. But sometimes your parents are smart, too.*

The very next day, my father and mother were smart. After breakfast (more squirrel), they looked at each other for a long time. I knew they had something planned.

"Luke, Isaac, we are going for a walk, without your mother," my father said. "Isaac, carry Jumper. Hold him tight and don't let him go."

We climbed out of the lean-to and walked away from the camp. We crossed the icy swamp, on the far side of the island.

"Careful," my father warned. "Do not fall through the ice!"

Jumper wiggled, trying to get free.

"I want to run," Jumper said. "Let me go!"

"Not yet," I told him.

We walked for almost an hour.

"Now," my father said, "let Jumper go. He's ready to run."

"You heard your father," Jumper said. "Let me down!"

I dropped him and Jumper took off running.

"I am faster than you are," Jumper called over his shoulder. I had to laugh. Of course, he was faster than me! I ran after him anyway. I tripped over a log covered in snow and rolled and tumbled.

"Be careful!" my father shouted.

When I came to my feet, my face was covered in snow. Luke laughed and pointed at me.

"You are a snow monster!" he said.

I didn't know what a snow monster was. I just knew I didn't like being called one. I grabbed a handful of snow and rolled a snowball.

Hoke. You are smart enough to know what I did next. I threw the snowball at Luke. He ducked and the snowball hit my father — in the face!

This was bad, real bad. I had never hit my father with a snowball. I stood and waited.

"Uh-oh," Luke said.

"Uh-oh," Jumper said.

We waited to see what my father would do. First he

29

stepped behind a tree. Luke and I looked at each other.

"This is strange," Jumper said.

The tree was covered in icicles and we heard cracking sounds. My father was breaking icicles from the branches. We stood still for a long time. What happened next was scary, really scary.

"Grrrr!" A low growling sound came from behind the tree.

"Grrrrrrrr!" The sound grew louder.

"I don't like this," Jumper said.

Without warning, something jumped from behind the tree!

"I am the real snow monster!" the thing yelled.

The snow monster wore my father's clothes. He had no hands. Icicles poked from his sleeves, where his fingers should be. And his head was made of snow.

The snow monster ran after us. He waved his arms and icicles flew all around us. He tackled Luke. They both rolled in the snow.

"Grrrr!" the thing yelled.

"Where is your father?" Jumper asked.

"No time for talking," I said. "Run!"

"Help!" Luke shouted.

"You are on your own," said Jumper. "I do not fight snow monsters!"

I thought the snow monster *was* my father, but Jumper and I didn't wait to see. We hid behind a big rock and clung to each other. The snow monster dragged Luke behind the tree. We heard more cracking sounds.

"Grrrrr!" That was the snow monster growling.

"Grrrrrrrr!" That sounded like Luke, growling *like* a snow monster.

"This has gone far enough," Jumper said.

I knew what was about to happen. Big Snow Monster jumped out: "Grrrr!"

When Little Snow Monster appeared, I laughed. It was scary, but I laughed anyway.

"Grrrrrr! I am Son of Snow Monster!" Little Snow Monster yelled.

Little Snow Monster was wearing Luke's clothes! His fingers were icicles and his head was a giant snowball.

"Hey, I want to be a snow monster!" I said.

Big Snow Monster looked at Little Snow Monster. I never knew snow monsters could shrug their shoulders. These two did.

"Come on," said Big Snow Monster.

We all went behind the tree, but Jumper stayed behind the rock. He was still scared and didn't want to be close to any snow monster.

My father (*hoke*, he was not a real snow monster) broke icicles from the tree. Luke (Little Snow Monster) scooped up enough snow to make me a snow monster head. I knew what we were about to do.

"Jumper likes to run," my father said. "We'll give him a good reason to run."

Jumper jumped on top of the rock.

"What's going on?" he asked.

We didn't answer. Soon I was ready, with icicle fingers and a snowy head.

"Grrrrr!" we growled from behind the tree.

"Go," my father whispered.

We jumped into the open.

"Grrrrrr!"

Jumper did not move. He was so afraid he just stared at us. Then he leapt from the rock and started running.

We waved our arms and flung icicles. We shook our heads and snow flew everywhere.

"Help!" shouted Jumper.

We chased Jumper through the trees and up a hill. I knew Jumper was fast, but he ran faster than ever! That's what happens when you're a dog being chased by three snow monsters.

Finally, Jumper stopped. Our icicle fingers were gone. Our snow heads were gone.

"Hey!" said Jumper. "That is not funny. You are not snow monsters. You are Luke, Isaac, and Father."

"I'm sorry, Jumper," I said. "We played a joke, that's all."

"Let's go home, now," my father said. "Jumper, we will make you something special for supper tonight."

"I think I deserve it," said Jumper. He was already wagging his tail. I knew he forgave us.

I learned something important that day. Hitting your father in the face with a snowball is not a good idea — unless you want to spend the rest of the day with real live Choctaw snow monsters.

I learned something else, too. Being a snow monster was better than being a ghost.

Chapter 8
Walking People

LUKE AND MY FATHER went hunting that afternoon. They returned with a deer! We roasted our first deer since leaving home. My mother gave Jumper the first piece of deer meat.

The next morning Old Man and Old Woman stayed in their lean-to. Most of our Choctaw friends stayed inside, too, curled up in their blankets. No one laughed.

By afternoon Choctaw people from every lean-to moaned and cried. Old people, young people, everyone cried. As day turned to darkness, a young girl shouted, "I am burning." Her mother ran to the swamp and brought her a cup of water.

"We should get a good night's sleep," my father said. "We will be leaving in the morning."

"Where will we go?" my mother asked.

"Away," my father answered. "Far away."

"I hate to leave our friends," Mother said.

"So do I," said my father. "But there is nothing we can do to help them."

I had a bad dream that night. I dreamed of what would happen in a few days. Old Man and Old Woman were covered in sores. They itched and burned and the sores never went away. Everyone with a blanket had the sores.

How did my mother know? I asked myself. *How did she know the blankets carried smallpox?*

Smallpox was a dark secret. It climbed from the blankets and carried the sores. I had already seen smallpox, but I didn't know it.

A week earlier, when I saw Old Man and Old Woman playing like children in the river, I saw smallpox. With my ghost eyes, I saw it.

Some Choctaws became ghosts from the shotguns. Some became ghosts from the burning houses. But the blankets made more ghosts than any guns or fires. The smallpox blankets were ghost-making blankets.

Our days in the swamp were over.

Early the next morning we gathered our belongings and left the camp. We walked all day and slept in the woods.

The next morning we came to a road. As far as we could see, Choctaw people were walking. Soldiers drove wagons and Choctaws walked. The roads were covered with snow and ice.

Most of the Choctaws had blankets wrapped around their shoulders. When my father saw the blankets he pulled us close. We followed this band of soldiers and walking Choctaws for three days, hiding in the tree shadows, unseen by anyone.

I carried Jumper so he couldn't chase the walking people. But he didn't even try to get away. After the *Nahullos* burned our town, Jumper knew when to be quiet. He seemed to understand about the ghosts, too, so I asked him.

"Do you see the ghosts, Jumper?"

"Do you promise not to tell?" he said.

"I won't tell anyone. I promise."

"Okay," said Jumper. "I see the ghosts. Maybe I will be a ghost soon."

"Jumper, no!"

Jumper just looked at me. I think he knew that I would soon be a ghost. We never spoke of it again.

On the morning of the fourth day, my father stepped out of the tree shadows and spoke to a friendly Choctaw man passing by.

"My family has no place to go," my father said. "Our town was burned and we have been living in the woods."

"You can come with us," the man said. "My name is Gabe. We are going to a new home, a home they will never take from us."

"The blankets?" my father asked. "Did the soldiers give you the blankets?" I knew what he was thinking. He was remembering the ghost-making blankets.

"Yes," Gabe said. "They are thick and warm."

My father nodded. "I am Zeke, and this is my wife, Ochi. These are my sons, Luke and Isaac."

"This is my wife, Ruth," said Gabe. "You are welcome to join us."

Ruth lifted her hand from under her blanket and waved. I couldn't see her face, but I could hear her laughing under her blanket.

"I am cooooold!" she said.

Ruth was short and round, and I knew she would be a funny friend. I saw something wiggling under her blanket.

"Momma!" a tiny voice said.

Ruth lifted her blanket and a little girl stood next to her.

"This is Nita," Ruth said.

Nita buried her face in the blanket.

"She is shy," said Ruth. "She is five years old."

"*Halito*, Nita!" we all said. She didn't look at us, but she waved.

"Just like her mother," Gabe said, and everybody laughed.

My family joined the walkers that day. After the burning of our town, the days in the swamp, and the blankets with small pox, my family joined the walkers. We were on our way to a new home.

But we were not alone.

Mister Jonah came to me the first night.

After sundown, Gabe and my father built a campfire close to the road. We had dried corn for our first night's meal. I was so hungry that I would have eaten the corn uncooked. But with wild onions, roasted over a log fire, it was delicious!

After supper we sat close to the fire.

"Do you want me to get you blankets?" Gabe asked my father. "The soldiers have blankets in the wagon."

"Not yet," my father said. "We will wait a few days."

We all slept close together. It was warmer that way. Sometime after midnight, when everyone else was asleep, I felt the warm shiver and sat up. The ghost of Mister Jonah sat next to me.

"We are waiting for you," he said.

"Did you die in the fire?"

"Yes, I did," he said. "But I am not alone. Missus Jonah is with me. Are you ready to come with us?"

"No," I told him. "I want to be with my family."

"You will be with us soon," he said, and stood to go.

"Wait," I said. "I want to ask you something."

"What?"

"Are the blankets safe?"

Mister Jonah smiled.

"Your mother was smart not to let you take a blanket in the swamp."

"But these new blankets," I asked, "are the new blankets safe?"

"Yes. The new blankets are safe."

"Thank you," I said. "I am glad you came."

After he was gone, I woke my father up.

"The blankets are safe," I whispered.

"How do you know?"

37

"I saw Mister Jonah. His ghost told me the new blankets are safe."

"I will ask for blankets in the morning," my father said.

Chapter 9

Nita and the Ghost Walkers

"HERE THEY ARE!" said Gabe. He plopped the blankets in front of my father. We still sat by the morning fire.

"*Yakoke*," said my mother. (*Yakoke* means "thank you" in Choctaw.) She unrolled the blankets and wrapped one around me.

"Here's one for you, too, Luke," she said, handing one to my brother. "And one for your father, and one for me!"

We sat looking at each other. My blanket itched, but I didn't care. I was with my family and we were warm. For the first time since our home burned, we were warm.

As we started the day's walk, the sun shone and the sky was clear and cloudless. The road was frozen and my feet were cold, but the sun felt good on my face.

We walked through a thick forest and melting icicles

fell all around us. A tree branch broke and fell to the ground. Nita squealed and jumped under my blanket!

"Can I walk with you?" she asked. Her tiny voice was so soft and muffled by the thick blanket.

"Yes, little Nita, you can walk with me," I said, giving her a big smile.

"I never had a big brother," she said. "Will you be my big brother?"

"Of course," I said. "I'd be happy to be your big brother."

That night at the campfire Nita suddenly stood. She walked close to the fire and turned to look at us.

"What are you doing?" her mother asked.

"I have something to say . . . to everybody," Nita said.

"What is it?" her mother asked.

"I have a big brother. Isaac is my new big brother."

I hung my head and hoped nobody would make fun of me. I thought this big-brother-thing would be a secret. I didn't look at Luke. If anybody laughed at me, it would be him.

I was wrong.

"Isaac will be a good big brother for you, Nita," Luke said. "I like being his big brother. He will like being yours."

I looked up. Luke was smiling at me.

"*Yakoke*," I said softly.

I looked around the circle. Everyone was staring at me, waiting for me to do something. This was a special time, but I didn't know what to do. I finally stood and walked over by Nita.

"I am proud to be your big brother, Nita," I said. "I will

take care of you." Everyone nodded and smiled, and Ruth started singing the Choctaw friendship song. We all joined in, and for the first time our two families felt like one.

I hoped I could keep my promise, my promise to take care of Nita. Later that night, just before I fell asleep, I had a funny thought.

If I am a ghost, how can I take care of Nita? I asked myself.

By morning, I knew what to do. I could take care of Nita, as best I could, while I was still alive. I ate my breakfast in a hurry, and while everyone else was eating, I found a sharp stone. I cut two small pieces from my blanket.

"Nita, let me see your feet," I said. Nita lay back on her mother's lap and lifted her feet high. I tied the blanket pieces on her feet.

"Now," I said, "your feet will be warm when you walk. No more walking on icy roads, not for *my* little sister!"

I was glad Nita now had warm blanket shoes. That afternoon the wind blew hard and the sky was covered with mean, icy clouds.

"We should find a tree to sleep under tonight," Gabe said. "I think bad weather is coming."

We built our campfire under an old oak tree with thick branches.

Gabe was right. The next morning a hard rain fell. A clap of thunder woke me up, but my blanket was already soaking wet. I stood under the tree and shivered. I tried shaking the water from my blanket.

A soldier rode his horse into our camp.

41

"No time to build a fire," he said. "Breakfast will have to wait. We need to move. Start walking. If the rain stops, you can build the cooking fires."

"Careful!" my father shouted. "The roads will be slippery!"

I could barely hear his voice above the pounding rain. Soon the rain turned to ice. By late morning, the world was covered in ice. We walked without stopping all day, with nothing to eat.

An hour before sunset the sleet stopped. The woods were thick on both sides of the road. Long icicles hung from every tree branch. The soldier rode up and down the line of Choctaw walkers, shouting, "Let's make camp here!"

We found a small clearing in a clump of trees and started building our evening fire. By now we were like one big family. Gabe, Ruth, and Nita were more than friends. They were family. We shared the work and then we shared the food.

A soldier dropped off a bag of corn for our supper.

"Milk will be here, soon," he said. In a few minutes, another soldier brought a jug of milk.

"Thank you," Gabe said. "Where did you get the milk?"

"We bought it from a nearby farmer," said the soldier.

"I hope that farmer has a lot of cows," Gabe said, after the soldier left. "We need milk for a thousand Choctaws!"

We had Choctaw corn soup for supper that night. *Pashofa*, we call it. Soft corn in milk chowder. Yummm!

The next morning I remembered what Gabe had said: "a thousand Choctaws."

As we started to walk, I felt the warm shiver. I was afraid to open my eyes. My two families surrounded me, and I didn't want to see anybody die.

"I do not want to know," I whispered to myself. Then I felt a warm hand on my cheek.

"It is me, Isaac." It was Mister Jonah's voice. I opened my eyes.

"I was scared," I told him. "Sometimes I know too much."

"I understand," said Mister Jonah. "I want this to be easy for you."

"How can dying be easy?" I asked.

"I cannot give you a good answer," he said. "But there is something you should see. Go ahead, look all around."

I pulled back my blanket and stretched my neck high. As far as I could see, Choctaws were beginning their walk for the day.

"I see this every day," I said.

Mister Jonah laughed. "You are not looking close enough."

I squinted my eyes. The shiver was so warm I felt as if I was sitting close to a fire. I saw the Choctaw walkers, like before. But now I saw hundreds more Choctaws. Choctaw ghost walkers.

"Where did these people come from?" I asked.

"They came from all over Choctaw country," he said. "They died from the fires. They died from sickness and they died from hunger. But they will never leave."

"They are like you?" I asked him.

"Yes, son. They are like me. We are here to help you. Our lives are over, but we can still help the living."

"Can I ever call for your help?" I asked.

"Isaac, I will be there when you need me." As soft and quiet as the moon rising, Missus Jonah appeared at his side.

"I am here for you, too," she said.

"Now," said Mister Jonah, "we should be going. Today will be hard for you. Know that we are here." I closed my eyes and they were gone.

"Isaac!" my father shouted. "Catch up!"

This day was the coldest day of our walk, colder even than our days in the swamp. Freezing rain fell all day long, and I could not forget what Mister Jonah had said.

"Today will be hard for you."

I wondered what he meant.

I soon had my answer.

Chapter 10

Bloody Footprints

WHEN WE STOPPED for our noon meal, everyone huddled close to the fire. Everyone but me. I wasn't hungry and I was so cold I couldn't stop shaking. I stood under a tree, away from the icy rain.

"You should warm yourself by the fire," my mother said.

I was too cold to move.

"It is dry here," I said.

"Lift your feet," my father said. "You should move. You will never get warm standing there."

I covered my head with my blanket and leaned against the tree. I was standing in a pool of ice. I looked up and the snow was so thick I could not see the tree limbs. Nothing but white falling snowflakes.

"Come on!" my father shouted. "Time to walk."

I didn't move. *Maybe now is my time*, I thought. *Maybe that is what Mister Jonah was telling me. Maybe today I will become a ghost.*

I felt a tug on my hand.

"Come with us," Nita said.

"You better walk with your mother," I said. If I was about to be a ghost, I didn't want Nita to see.

I wiped the snow from my eyes. The camp was empty and everyone was gone. I took a step. I had been standing for an hour. My father had warned me.

"Lift your feet!" he had said.

I should have listened.

Mister Jonah had warned me, too.

"Today will be hard for you."

I tried to walk, but my feet were frozen to the ground. I pulled and tugged, and when I finally lifted my right foot, the skin tore away.

"Owwww!" I hollered. Pain shot up my leg and hot tears filled my eyes. I rocked back and forth, but the pain wouldn't go away.

"Come on, Isaac," Luke called to me. "You are falling behind!"

I clenched my jaw and raised my left foot, as gently as I could. I had sunk so deep in the ice, the skin of that foot ripped away, too. I jumped from one foot to the other. My feet were freezing cold and burning hot at the same time. I never knew pain could hurt this bad.

"Please make this be over," I said out loud. I felt the warm shiver.

"If you are ready," Mister Jonah said.

"You are welcome with us," Old Man said.

"It is warm here," Old Woman said.

I closed my eyes and wished everything to go away.

When I opened them, I saw everyone who had taken a blanket: Choctaw children, boys and girls, and men and women, too. They all stood before me, floating in a puffy white cloud. No one wore any blankets and their sores were gone. The sun shone on a beautiful blue sky. I knew I was seeing a ghost world.

"You will like it with us," said a young man.

"No!" I shouted. "No! I am not ready!"

I shook my head and they were gone. One step at a time I started walking. The snow was thick and my feet stung with every step. I looked behind me.

I was leaving bloody footprints in the snow. Mounds of snow covered the road. The snow fell in soft white flakes, but now the snow behind me was dotted red. I walked ahead, but I could not stop myself from looking over my shoulder.

Ten steps, ten bloody footprints. A hundred steps, a hundred bloody footprints trailing after me. I wanted to run, to leave the footprints behind me.

I did run, but the footprints followed me. The faster I ran, the more footprints.

"Make them go away!" I shouted.

"It is time," said Mister Jonah.

"No! I don't want to go with you!" I shouted. My voice was hoarse from shouting.

Then another voice cut through the snow.

"Son!" It was my father's voice.

The Choctaw ghosts vanished. Far ahead my father waited. I stumbled and fell and my father ran to meet me. He picked me up and held me close.

"Isaac," he said, "take one last look behind you."

I turned my head and saw my footprints in the snow.

"Son," he said, "you cannot keep your eyes on the bloody footprints you have left behind you. You must keep your eyes on where you are going."

I took a deep breath. I nodded. From that moment on, even though my feet burned, I refused to look behind me. I looked where I was going and forgot about the pain. I was stronger than the pain.

Three days later my feet healed. But the healing began when I heard my father say those words.

"You cannot keep your eyes on the bloody footprints you have left behind you. You must keep your eyes on where you are going."

Chapter 11

Nita's Walk

THE NEXT MORNING Nita woke me up, while the rest of the camp was still asleep.

"I have a gift for you," she said. She took her blanket shoes off and tied them to my feet.

"You need the shoes," she said. I had learned long ago never to refuse a gift.

"*Yakoke*, Nita," I said, smiling at my little sister. "You are sweet." Nita ran to the campfire and hid behind her mother.

"Nita, where are your shoes?" her mother asked.

Nita pointed to me.

"She wanted me to have these," I said. Her mother beamed with pride. I ate my breakfast quickly, then I cut Nita another pair of shoes.

"Here," I said to her. "Now big brother and little sister both have blanket shoes!"

"I like that!" she said.

Nita stayed near me all day. Once she jumped under my blanket and giggled. The cold was easier to endure with Nita close by.

At sunset the wind blew hard and rattled the ice in the trees. I drew my blanket over my head. Our day's walk would soon be over, and I was glad.

The shiver came swift and warm. I opened my eyes and Nita smiled at me. As I watched, her face swelled till her lips were puffy and her eyes were tiny slits. She stared at me without moving.

At first I didn't notice the small spider by her nose. It was a tiny black spider and it crawled across her face. I reached out a finger to flick it from her cheek, but my hand went right through her!

Nita was a ghost.

"It is her time," Mister Jonah whispered in my ear.

When I opened my eyes, Nita was still alive, walking beside her mother. We stepped from the road and into the woods. Luke and I gathered wood, while Gabe and my father started the cooking fire.

We all slept close to the fire. Nita slept by her mother and I found a dry spot on the ground next to Luke. When everyone else was asleep, I spoke to him. I had to talk to someone.

"Luke, are you awake?" I whispered.

"Yes," he said.

"Tomorrow will be a bad day."

"How do you know?" he asked.

"I just know," I said. "I am afraid for Nita."

"Can we help her?" he asked.

"No. I don't know how to help her."

"I am your brother, Isaac," Luke said. "Whatever happens, we are strong. We have seen many people die. We are some of the lucky ones. We still have our family."

"You are a good brother, Luke," I said, and drifted off to sleep.

The next morning, Ruth's cries woke everyone. Sometime during the night, Nita had rolled out of her blanket. She now lay covered by a blanket of snow, with only her face showing. I saw the tiny spider crawl across the face of my little sister, Nita.

"No," Ruth sobbed. "My sweet Nita, my little girl. No!"

My mother ran to help and wrapped Nita in her blanket. Nita did not move. She would never move again.

Ruth's cries carried far beyond our camp, and soon a dozen women circled Nita and her mother. The older women broke bark from the trunks of cedar trees. They burned the bark and waved the smoke over Nita. They sang the Choctaw death song.

No one built a cooking fire that morning.

A soldier rode his horse into camp.

"Time to walk!" he shouted. He looked at Nita and the women.

Another soldier pulled his horse to a stop.

"What's the hold up?" he asked.

"Another one died," the soldier said.

"One less to feed," said the second soldier.

They rode away.

I was glad Nita's family did not hear the soldiers' talk. But I had heard them, and Luke and my father heard them. We would never forget what they said.

Chapter 12

Disappearing Daughter

I HAD NEVER SEEN anybody as sad as Ruth and Gabe were that morning. Nobody said a word. Ruth knelt on the ground and wrapped Nita in her blanket. Gabe helped her to her feet and Ruth took the first step, carrying her little girl's body.

Gabe clung to her arm, as if he was afraid of falling. The women followed and the walk began.

I had never seen a parent lose a child before. I was seeing something else, too. I now knew what my parents would feel when I became a ghost. I felt the warm shiver coming.

"No, not now," I said. I closed my eyes tight and shook my head.

"Do not be afraid," a tiny voice said to me. "You are

still my big brother." I opened my eyes and Nita stood before me.

"I am sorry," I said. "I wanted to help you."

"You can help me," Nita said. "You can help my mother and father, too. You can make them happy again."

"How can I do that?"

"You can find my sister."

"Your sister?" I asked. "I didn't know you had a sister."

"Ask my father about her," Nita said. She smiled at me and reached for my hand. "He will tell you." Then she was gone.

Nita had another sister? If she was lost, why weren't they looking for her?

I knew this was a secret not even my mother or father knew.

I had to be very careful.

We made camp early that day. Ruth and Gabe traded carrying Nita, and they barely lifted their feet when they walked. Their feet left a sad trail on the road. Sometimes they sang the death song; sometimes they sang *Amazing Grace* in Choctaw. It is our song.

After our corn soup supper, I watched Gabe. I knew it would be easier to talk to him alone. When he stood up to go to the woods, I followed.

"Gabe, can we talk?" I asked.

"Yes, if you want to."

"I want to help."

"What can you do?" he said. I knew he was not listening, not yet.

"I want to help you find your other daughter."

The look on his face changed. He looked almost angry.

"We do not have another daughter," he said. "Do not speak of this!"

"Gabe, I know this is a secret. I have told no one."

"What are you talking about?" he said. I saw that he was no longer angry. He was afraid.

"Nita told me."

He started crying and moaning. "Go away, please."

"I want to help," I said. "Nita told me about her. Gabe, I have a secret, too. This is a secret my mother and father do not know."

"What is your secret?"

"I will be a ghost," I told him. "Soon, I think."

Gabe grabbed my shoulder. He turned me around and looked me in the eyes. "I am listening," he said.

"I see ghosts. They tell me things. Nita came to me this morning after she died. She wants me to find her sister. She wants you to be happy again."

"Nita told you this?"

"Yes."

"I cannot talk to you about Nita's sister. Not yet. I need to ask Ruth. Then maybe we can talk."

"What can I tell Nita?" I asked. "You know she won't let this go."

For the first time since Nita died and became a ghost, Gabe smiled. His body shook and his eyes filled with tears, but he was smiling.

"You are right," he said. "She is a determined little girl.

Tonight we can talk. All of us, your family, too."

"*Yakoke*. Gabe, I miss her, too." He patted me on the shoulder and we walked back to camp. I couldn't stop myself from listening as he spoke to Ruth.

"No, no, we cannot do this," Ruth said. He pulled her close and they spoke in whispers, till Ruth looked at me with a question in her eyes.

The wind blew strong that day. The snow swirled in circles and we were blinded by it. As I walked, I looked to my feet and pulled the blanket over my head.

If I walk off the road I'll bump into a tree, I thought. *That's how I will know I'm off the road.*

When you cannot see, your mind tells strange stories.

Maybe that's how it happens, I thought. *That is how I become a ghost. I bump into a tree and icicles fall all around me. I slip and fall. Then one long dagger icicle waits for its turn to fall. Everybody in the world stares at that one giant icicle. They hold their breath. I look at the icicle, too.*

I realize I am lying right under it.

"No," I whisper. The icicle responds.

It shakes, but it keeps everybody waiting. It is a very cruel icicle; anybody can see that. Then, as if it has nothing better to do, the icicle falls. I close my eyes. The icicle stabs me in the heart!

"No!" I shouted.

I was in the real world.

"Isaac," my father said, grabbing me. "Are you *hoke*?"

"Yes. I just had a bad dream while I was walking."

"That's okay," he said. "I have been having bad walking

56

dreams all day, too. Stay strong. This will be over soon."
Not until I am a ghost, I thought.
But I couldn't tell him that.
Not yet.

Chapter 13

The Coming of My Final Day

BY NIGHTFALL THE snow stopped, but the air turned bitter and cold. After supper, Gabe scooted close to the fire and everyone gathered to listen.

"We should talk about something," he said. Ruth had her blanket wrapped tight so no one could see her face. She began to shake and sob.

"Ruth is afraid," Gabe said. "But we have nothing to fear now. They can't hurt us anymore."

My mother and father looked at each other but said nothing.

"Now that Nita is gone," Gabe continued, "they can't hurt us."

"Who would want to hurt you?" my father asked.

"The soldiers. They said they would take Nita away if

we told anybody what I am about to tell you. We have another daughter. Her name is Naomi and she is twelve years old."

"Where is she?" my mother asked.

"The soldiers took her," Gabe said. "They rode into our camp one morning. They were looking for someone to do their cooking. A soldier spotted Naomi and threw her on his horse. Naomi is a strong young girl. She kicked and screamed. I ran to help her, but the soldier knocked me to the ground with his shotgun. 'We are taking her!' the soldier shouted.

"Then he fired his shotgun at a branch over my head. I jumped away just in time and the branch fell at my feet. The soldier didn't care. 'She is ours now,' he said.

"Then he looked at Nita. 'If you want to keep your other daughter, say nothing about this. If you say a word to anybody, we will come for this little girl, too. You will never see either of them alive again.' "

No one said anything for a long time. Ruth buried her face in her hands and cried quietly. Finally, my mother spoke.

"Do you know where Naomi is?" she asked.

"No," Gabe said. "We have been afraid to look, afraid to ask or tell anyone what happened. But now that Nita is gone, they cannot hurt us anymore." Then he looked at me.

"Isaac has something to tell you," he said.

Everybody was looking at me. I was embarrassed, but I knew that the time had come for me to tell my mother and father, and Luke, too, my own secret.

"Please don't anybody be mad at me," I began. "I don't want to upset anyone. Losing our home was bad enough."

"What do you need to tell us, son?" my father asked.

"I will soon be a ghost."

There. I'd said it. I closed my eyes. I felt the warm shiver. When I opened them, I was surrounded by Choctaw ghosts. Nita, Mister and Missus Jonah, Old Man and Old Woman. They stood in a circle around me. But there were more, at least a hundred other ghosts, many I did not know. They smiled and nodded.

"We are proud of you, Isaac," Old Man said. "We know this is not easy, but they needed to know."

I closed my eyes again. When I reopened them, everybody was waiting and the ghosts were gone.

"I don't know how, but it will be soon." I looked at my mother. She was trying hard not to cry. I knew she wanted to be strong for me.

"Ghosts come to me," I said. "They show me things, things that are about to happen. That is how I knew Mister and Missus Jonah burned in the fire. I saw their hair on fire that day by the river. I saw Old Man and Old Woman covered in sores. But I don't know what happened to their grandson, Joseph.

"Nita came to me yesterday," I continued. "She told me about her sister. She said she would help me find her."

I looked at Gabe and Ruth. "She wants you to be happy again," I told them.

"What can we do to help?" my father asked.

"I don't know," I said, "but the ghosts will tell me. If I have to leave camp to find her, you must understand. Please don't try to stop me."

"Will you be safe, son?" my mother asked.

Her question floated above the campfire. No one wanted to say what everyone was thinking.

He can be safe, but it will not matter. Isaac will be dead soon. He will join the others. He will be a ghost.

No one said it, but that is what everyone was thinking.

I did not have long to wait. I thought the ghost world was full of surprises, but the biggest surprise of my life woke me up that night.

"Isaac," a voice whispered. I rubbed my eyes. The sky was dark, and morning was still several hours away.

Somebody was leaning over me, but all I could see was a shadow surrounded by the bright moonlight. This was not a ghost. I was sure of that.

"Who is it?" I asked.

"It's me, Joseph. Old Man and Old Woman were my grandparents," the shadow said.

I sat up. Jumper sat up, too. He didn't bark. He knew who it was, and now that I could see him better, I recognized Joseph. He was older than me, maybe thirteen or fourteen.

"Where have you been?" I asked.

"It's a long story," Joseph said. "I'll tell you later. Right now, we need to find Naomi."

"Do you know where she is?" I asked.

"Yes, and she is still alive," he said. "The soldiers still

have her. But getting her back will not be easy. They are the meanest soldiers of all. They are the soldiers that brought the bad blankets."

I was afraid now, more afraid than ever. If these soldiers still had the blankets, we could all die.

"What can we do?" I asked.

"First, let your mother and father know you are leaving. We don't want them to be worried when they wake up and you are gone. Then let's go somewhere where we can talk."

I crawled to my father.

"Dad, wake up," I said in a quiet voice. I didn't want to wake my mother.

"What is it?" my mother asked.

She never sleeps, I thought. *No keeping secrets from her, not for a minute.*

My father rolled over and mumbled something.

"Wake up," my mother said, shaking my father.

"I have to go now," I told them. "I think I know where Naomi is. Don't worry. I'll come back as soon as I can."

"Be careful, son," my father said.

"I will. I promise," I said, but I was worried. I knew I might never see them again, not as a living person. My day of becoming a ghost grew closer, I could feel it.

Chapter 14

Joseph's Story

I FOLLOWED JOSEPH to a small clearing in the woods.

"Now," he said. "It's safe to talk. We have to be very quiet. No one can know where we are, not even Choctaws. This will be dangerous. You should know that."

"I understand," I said.

"Good. The soldiers took Naomi to a wagon, one of the wagons that brought the blankets into the swamp that morning."

"Did you take a blanket that morning Joseph?" I asked. I had to know. If he took a blanket, if he had wrapped himself in the blanket, we might both be dying soon.

"No," he said. "I was hunting that morning. When the soldiers left the swamp, they saw me. I had caught three squirrels and was headed back to camp. I tried to run, but I slipped on the ice." He pulled back his hair. "Look at this."

Over his right ear was a deep cut.

"Does it hurt?" I asked.

"Not anymore, but it bled for a long time. The soldiers let me lay there, bleeding in the snow. They made their camp for the evening, and by the time I woke up, they were cooking my squirrels for their supper. Then one of the soldiers saw I was awake.

" 'Are you cold, Indian?' he asked me. I told him, Yes. He brought me a blanket. It was one of the bad blankets, the ones that made everybody sick. I would have taken it. But another soldier stopped him. I guess the second soldier saved my life.

" 'Wait,' the second soldier said. 'This boy can help us. Let's keep him alive.'

"They threw me in the rear of the wagon. They tied my hands and feet together. 'If you try to get away, we will shoot you,' they said.

"I knew the time to escape would come, but I wanted to win their trust. For several days I did everything they asked me to do. I built their cooking fires.

" 'If you set me on a rock by the water, I will catch fish for you,' I told them. 'You can keep my feet tied. I won't run away.'

"I caught enough catfish for everybody. They even let me have a few bites. I was starving.

"After a week, they started to trust me. I could tell. They let me eat with them. They didn't yell at me in their mean voices. One night after supper, a soldier asked me,

'Do you want to go home to your parents?'

" 'No,' I said. 'They are fine without me.'

"The soldiers laughed at me. 'You are so dumb!' they said. 'Your parents are dead. The blankets we gave them had smallpox. It kills. All the Choctaws are dead, boy. You are the only one left alive.'

"They laughed and laughed. They meant my grandparents, but they didn't know. And that did not matter. They had just told me that everyone in my town was dead, and they were laughing."

Joseph paused. I knew he was ready to stop talking for a while. I knew he was remembering his grandparents, Old Man and Old Woman.

"How did you escape?" I finally asked him.

"I told the biggest lie of my life," Joseph said. "I told them, 'Thank you for saving my life.' I did not feel grateful to them. I didn't know if I wanted to stay alive or not. I was so angry. I wanted to kill them."

Joseph grew quiet. He closed his eyes and I knew he was lost in his own thoughts. He moved closer to me and put his hand on my shoulder.

"Can I trust you?" he asked.

"Yes," I said. "Why are you asking me that?"

"Because what I am about to tell you is known by very few people. My grandparents knew, and they kept the secret."

"I will tell no one," I promised.

"Then I'll tell you how I escaped. The next day they took me fishing again. They had to carry me to the river. My feet were still tied, tight. They checked the ropes several times a day. I caught enough fish for everybody and limped back to camp, carrying the fish. I also carried something else, a sharp stone.

"I knew the best time to escape was at night. After supper, I waited till I heard snoring. I had to make sure everybody was asleep. I knew they would kill me if they caught me. I cut the ropes with the stone and I ran.

"I didn't look over my shoulder. I ran faster than I had ever run in my life. I ran first to the river. The moon shone bright and I could see where I was going. I didn't stop running till morning. Then I hid in a small cave, on a hill overlooking the river.

"They must have followed my footprints in the snow. I thought I was free, but no. I heard the horses snorting below me. Just as the sun was rising, I peeked from the cave and saw the soldiers climbing the hill on horseback. I knew the time had come. My life depended on it."

Joseph paused and took a deep breath. "I made the change," he said, in a low whisper. "I closed my eyes tight shut. I wrapped my arms around myself. I felt claws digging into my ribs. My claws. I was the panther. I was still myself. But now I had the body of a panther."

Joseph waited for me to say something. I dropped my jaw. I didn't know what to say. I had heard of panther people, but I had always thought the stories were not real. When he saw I believed him, he continued.

"The soldiers rode closer, almost to the mouth of the cave. I saw them reach for their rifles, and I knew I couldn't wait any longer. I leapt from the cave and knocked a soldier from his horse. I stood on my hind paws, waved my claws at them, and growled. I showed them my sharp teeth.

"They froze for just a moment, long enough for me to jump back in the cave.

" 'Let's get out of here!' shouted a soldier. 'If the boy is in the cave, he's dead by now.'

"They turned down the hill and rode away. I waited till dark, then I ran some more. I ran like only a panther can run. I didn't know where to go. I only wanted to be as far away from the soldiers as I could get. I was so afraid. That night I dreamed about my grandparents.

"The next day I became myself again. I stumbled through the woods to the road. I saw the wagons and the Choctaws walking ahead of me. I followed behind, keeping to the woods. I have been following the Choctaw walkers since that day."

"Is that how you found Naomi?" I asked.

"Yes. I walked up and down the trail, hiding in the trees. I wanted to be able to see the soldiers before they spotted me. I knew they would kill me on sight. One night I located their wagon. I crept close.

"They were all sitting around the campfire, laughing about the dumb Indian boy that thought he could get away. 'He ran right into the cave of a panther!' they said. 'By now that panther is gnawing on his bones!'

"I ran to the rear of the line. I followed from the shadows of the woods, and no soldiers knew I was there. Of course, some Choctaws saw, but they said nothing.

"I walked close to Gabe and Ruth's family, long before you came. They had two daughters, as you know, little Nita and her big sister, Naomi. One morning the soldier who had caught me rode into their camp. You know what happened next. They took Naomi. They told Gabe and Ruth that they would take Nita, too, if they tried to get Naomi back."

"So now that Nita is gone," I said, "they can't hurt her anymore."

"That's right," said Joseph. "We have nothing to fear."

He smiled when he said that. Of course, we had everything to fear. The soldiers could kill anybody they wanted, at any time they wanted. But we didn't fear for Nita. She was a ghost. She could take care of herself now.

Chapter 15

The Bending Branch of Treaty Talk

"I LEARNED SOMETHING else," Joseph said. "Our leaders are with us."

"What do you mean?" I asked him.

"Not every Choctaw is walking. Behind the lead wagons, there is another wagon. Choctaw councilmen ride in this wagon. It is not big enough for all of them, so some walk while the others ride. They switch out several times a day, when someone is too tired to walk.

"They can't know everything the soldiers do, but they watch them. That is why the soldiers bring us milk and corn. They have to feed us. They have to keep us safe."

"Why?" I asked.

"That is what the treaty says," Joseph said. "They have to take us safely to our new home in the west. That was what they agreed, at the Treaty Talk."

"I wish I never heard of Treaty Talk," I said. "Before Treaty Talk, we had our homes. With no Treaty Talk, Old Man and Old Woman would still be alive, and Nita and Mister and Missus Jonah, too."

Joseph lowered his eyes and looked away without responding. I wished I hadn't mentioned his grandparents, Old Man and Old Woman. I could see it made him sad to think of them, burning in the fire.

"What should we do?" I finally asked.

"We should help Naomi escape. The soldiers cut her hair. They make her wear boy's clothes. She does everything for them, just like I did. She cooks their meals. She washes their clothes. She feeds their horses."

"Do you have a plan?"

"Yes," Joseph replied. "The best plan of all. We wait. We stay close and watch and we wait."

"We wait for a sign," I said.

"Yes," he said. "You are a smart young man."

"Do you know about me?" I had to ask him.

Joseph smiled and nodded. "Yes," he said. "Why do you think I wanted your help? Your brother, Luke, is bigger and faster. I asked you to help because you see ghosts. And a ghost will bring you a sign."

We did not have long to wait.

I followed Joseph to a creek a half-mile from camp. We found a tree with thick limbs hanging almost to the ground. He grabbed the lowest limb and swung himself from one limb to the next till he was out of sight.

"Come on up," he said. "Nobody can see us here." I gripped the limb and was about to climb, when the warm shiver came.

"Come on," Joseph said. "Here, I'll help you."

His hand reached down for me, but all I could see was a cloudy mist. Old Man appeared before me.

"Isaac, I am worried for my grandson. You must warn Joseph. He must be very careful. The soldiers are waiting for him. They know he is here."

"We want to find Naomi," I said.

"You must go alone, Isaac. They will not hurt you. Go to the Choctaw Council wagon. Tell them your father sent you to help them. Joseph can stay in the woods. He can look out for you, but he must not be seen."

"What should I do?"

"While you are working, keep an eye out for Naomi. I will be there." As suddenly as he appeared, Old Man was gone. I looked at Joseph, sitting on a tree limb.

"You saw a ghost, didn't you?" he said.

"Yes. It was your grandfather."

"What did he say?"

I climbed the tree before I spoke. What I said was too important to yell out loud, for anyone to hear. When I sat next to him, I spoke in a whisper.

"Joseph, your grandfather is scared for you. He told me to warn you. The soldiers know you are here."

"How can they know that?"

"I don't know, but your grandfather is speaking the

71

truth. He is a ghost. He sees thing people can't see."

"We are going to rescue Naomi," Joseph said. "Did you tell him that? I wish I could talk to him."

"Yes, I told him. He has a plan." I told Joseph about me helping the Choctaw councilmen, in the wagon close to Naomi.

"I'll stay close, as close as I can," Joseph said. Then he bowed his head and spoke in a quiet and serious voice.

"I know these soldiers," he said. "I know what they will do. Isaac, when you see them, when you get close to them, remember they are the same men who burned our houses down while we slept inside. They tried to burn us all, burn us alive. And when that didn't work, they acted so kind and gave us blankets. The blankets killed most of our friends."

"I know. I remember," I said. "I try not to be afraid, Joseph, but I am more afraid than I've ever been in my life."

"And you are smart to be," he said, lifting his eyes to mine.

We climbed down the tree and made our way through the woods. Thinking of Joseph's warning, I stayed in the shadows, moving as quietly as I could from one clump of trees to the next.

"Be careful how you step," Joseph whispered. "The soldiers send out patrols. If they hear the leaves rattle, they won't wait to see what it is. They'll fire their shotguns. Nothing would make them happier than to kill two Choctaw boys sneaking through the woods."

The forest was thick with snaking vines and bushes at

the base of the trees. I knew no Choctaw farmers had ever lived here. By nightfall we neared the council wagon.

"*Hoke*," Joseph said, pointing to the wagon. "Here's where you take over."

"Joseph, don't say that! I need you now more than ever."

"Sorry," he said. "I'll be right with you, invisible as a ghost," he joked.

I stepped from the woods to the camp. Ten older Choctaw men and women sat by the fire, eating bowls of *pashofa*. A thin man with gray hair stood when I entered the camp.

"*Halito*," he said. "Welcome to our camp."

"*Yakoke*," I replied.

"I am Nani Humma, and these are my fellow Choctaw councilmen," he said, gesturing to the circle of people.

"My name is Isaac," I replied. "I am from a small town in the swamps to the south. I would like to offer my help. I can gather wood, make a fire. I can hunt and fish if you need me to."

The councilmen laughed.

"We get our food from the supply wagon," said Nani Humma. He was smiling, but I could see he was trying his best not to laugh at me. I liked him already. "Do you have family on the walk?" he asked.

"Yes, my mother and father and a big brother."

"They will be worried about you, Isaac," Nani Humma said. "You should let them know where you are."

"My parents gave me permission to leave our camp," I said. I hated lying to Nani Humma. And although I hadn't really told a lie, I was not telling him the whole truth. I decided to tell him everything, as soon as I could.

"Isaac," said Nani Humma. "*Yakoke* for your kind offer. If you will wait by the wagon, we need to talk for a few minutes."

I moved to the road and stood by the wagon. I watched as the councilmen huddled together. They spoke quietly, and I knew they were deciding what to do about me. After only a few minutes, Nani Humma stood and waved.

"*Hoke*, Isaac," he said. I stood before the Choctaw Council. I knew this was an important day for me.

"We have decided that you can join us," Nani Humma said.

"*Yakoke*," I said, nodding to everyone. "I will show you every respect."

I was greeted with warm smiles as I walked from one to another. They each took my hand and said nice things to me. I felt welcomed.

"Have you had supper yet?" Nani Humma asked.

"Let me get you a bowl of soup," said a councilwoman.

"Please," I said. "I am here to help you. Let me serve myself."

The councilmen laughed again, a laugh that let me know they were glad I was there. After supper, I took the bowls to the creek and washed them clean. I scattered the logs and put out the fire. I even helped a very old man to his feet.

Nani Humma gave me a thick blanket. "You can sleep by the fire," he said. "If it rains, we have a small tent by the wagon. Climb inside and sleep by the door."

For a brief moment, I wished everything was different. I wished I was not on a mission to rescue Naomi. I wished I were the helper of the Choctaw Council, not a boy who would soon be a ghost. *Maybe I can be a Choctaw councilman someday*, I thought.

Then I returned to the real world. *I could never be a Choctaw councilman. They would never elect a ghost to be a councilman.*

I hoped that my first night with the Choctaw Council would be peaceful. But that was not to be. Nani Humma was smarter than I thought. He knew I had a secret, and it didn't take him long to learn the truth.

Chapter 16

Seeking Naomi

I THOUGHT everyone was asleep. I'd heard old men snoring. But not every old man snores. I thought I had fooled them all, and anyway I had to talk to Joseph. I climbed from my blanket and walked to the creek.

"Joseph?" I whispered. "Are you here?"

"Yes," he said, stepping from behind a big cypress tree. "Good job."

"Isaac, who is your friend?" In the quiet woods of night, the voice of Nani Humma boomed like a shotgun. I jumped like I was the target.

Nani Humma stepped from the shadows. I hung my head and said nothing.

"I already know Isaac, but we have not met," said Nani Humma, stepping to Joseph and offering his hand.

Joseph and I stood still, ashamed and caught.

"I won't wake up the council, not at this late hour," said Nani Humma. "But you will tell me what is going on, and you will tell me now."

Joseph and I told Nani Humma the whole story. For almost an hour we talked. We told him of the burning of our homes. Joseph told of his escape. We told him about Naomi and our mission to rescue her. We told him of the soldiers, and how Joseph's life was in danger. I even told him about seeing the ghosts.

When I saw that he believed us, I told him my biggest secret.

"I will soon be a ghost," I said in a whisper. I looked at Nani Humma, hoping he would believe me. He said nothing, but he nodded to let me know he understood.

When we finished talking, Nani Humma sat in silence for the longest time. Finally he stood up, brushed the leaves from his pants, and spoke.

"The hour is late and we need our sleep. Isaac, you can stay with us for now. Joseph, as long as you cause no trouble, you are welcome, too. I don't think I have to tell you how important it is that you stay out of sight."

"I understand," Joseph said.

"*Yakoke*," I replied.

The next morning Nani Humma told the Choctaw Council about our nighttime visit. I finished serving breakfast and sat down to listen. When Nani Humma came to the part about Naomi, and how she had been taken, the councilmen gave fire to their anger.

"They took a young girl from her family?"

"They use her like a slave!"

"Her family thought she was dead! How horrible."

When everyone had had their say, Mister Tibbi stood to speak. He was the head of the council and a large man, thick as a tree trunk. Gray hair fell about his face and down his shoulders.

"If we approach these soldiers and accuse them of keeping this girl against her will, they will lie," he said. "The girl will be afraid of what they will do to her and her family if she tells the truth. She might never see her family again, or worse, she might disappear."

"What do you suggest we do?" Nani Humma asked.

"If Naomi is ever to return to her family, I think her best chance lies with these young men, our new helper, Isaac, and his friend Joseph. We can lend a hand when needed. We can keep an eye out for the girl. But we must do these things in secret. We cannot endanger our people."

There were nods all around.

Joseph and I stood a little straighter. Rescuing Naomi gave us all a purpose. I noticed it right away.

The councilwomen walked faster than usual that morning, leaving our wagon behind. When we stopped for our noon meal, the women kept walking. They waved to the soldiers, saying, "We know there are berries in these woods. If we find any, we'll make berry pudding. It's an old Choctaw recipe. You will love it!"

The soldiers smiled and waved back.

"We'll hold you to that promise!" the soldiers shouted.

I knew better than to follow the women, not on my first full day with the council, but I listened and heard the friendly talk.

These councilwomen are smart, I thought. *They are gaining the soldiers' trust.*

While I built the fire that evening, the women reported to the council.

"We saw her," said Stella. She was the eldest, a white-haired, thin woman. "We saw Naomi. When she heard us speaking to the soldiers, she peeked around the back of the wagon. She was curious, but I could tell she did not want us to see her."

"She is afraid for her family," said Nani Humma. "The soldiers said they would harm her little sister if she caused any trouble."

"She was dressed like a boy," Stella said, "just like we expected. But anyone who looked closely could see she is a strong young girl."

"A terrified young girl," said another woman.

"What do you think we should do now?" Nani Humma asked.

"Let the boys do their job," said Mister Tibbi.

Chapter 17

Good-bye to My Family

WHEN I BROUGHT Joseph his supper that night, Nani Humma followed me. We sat in the shadows till Joseph finished eating. Nani Humma was waiting for the evening report.

"Did you see Naomi today?" he asked.

"Yes," Joseph said. "She stayed close to the wagon. A soldier gathered firewood and lit the fire. Naomi cooked the meals."

"Does she ever go to the woods, maybe to the creek to wash the dishes?" Nani Humma asked.

"No, never," said Joseph. "They brought a bucket of water from the creek for dishwashing. During the day she stays inside the wagon. She never walks with the others. After supper, she climbed in the wagon to sleep. I saw a soldier climb in after her. He had a rope. I am sure she is tied up every night and released every morning."

"Is there a guard?" Nani Humma asked.

"Yes," Joseph said, "but he fell asleep sometime around midnight. The soldier that relieved him saw that he was sleeping. He kicked him awake and they laughed about it. They are not worried about us."

"And why should they worry?" Nani Humma said. "They have the guns."

"I can sneak past the guard," Joseph said. "This will not be as hard or dangerous as we thought. I still have my sharp stone, good for cutting ropes."

Nani Humma did not reply. Finally, he leaned in my direction. "What do you say, young Isaac?"

I knew what I thought, but I didn't like disagreeing with my best friend.

"Go on," Nani Humma said. I knew we were thinking the same thing.

"Well," I stammered, "I am worried about Naomi. If we try to rescue her, she might not want to go."

"Why not?" Joseph asked.

"She thinks Nita is alive," I said. "She is afraid of hurting her. She could scream and fight and wake the soldiers up."

"Then I am one dead Choctaw," Joseph said.

Nani Humma laughed softly. "Between the two of you, I think Naomi will be fine. I am impressed. And let's meet again tomorrow night. Be very careful tomorrow. Joseph, you stay away from the soldiers' camp. We don't want to risk you being seen. Isaac, why don't you and Joseph walk backwards tomorrow?"

We laughed for the first time in days!

"Why would we want to do that?" I asked. "It's a long enough walk without doing it backwards!"

"I think he means we should visit your folks tomorrow," said Joseph.

"Good thinking," Nani Humma said over his shoulder on his way back to camp. "It's been a long day for everyone. Let's get some sleep."

I liked Nani Humma. He was a powerful and important Choctaw, but he still had a sense of humor.

Joseph snuck into camp long before sunrise.

"Time to go," he whispered. I rolled up my blanket and put it in the back of the wagon.

"What about breakfast?" I asked. "I need to start the fire."

"Nani Humma will tell them where you are. Come on!"

I followed him to the river. We walked in the trees so no one would spot us. With Joseph in the lead, walking backwards was faster than I thought. After only an hour, we saw my family.

I was so happy to see them! My mother and father looked strong, and Luke looked very bored.

That's a good sign, I thought. *That means there is no trouble.*

"There they are," I told Joseph. "But where is Jumper?"

"Right behind you," Jumper said.

I turned around and Jumper jumped in my arms.

"What took you so long?" he said, licking my face with his sloppy wet tongue. I lifted Jumper over my head.

"I missed you Jumper," I said. "But I did not miss your tongue!"

I set him to the ground and Jumper ran circles around us, barking.

"Look at you," my father said. Joseph stayed in the shadows while I hugged my family, even Luke.

"I'm glad to see you're safe," Luke said.

"Are you here to stay?" my mother asked.

"No, only for a short visit," I said. "I made friends with the Choctaw councilmen. I'm their helper."

I had no way of knowing how short this visit would be. This was the last time I would ever see my family. At least, the last time *the living me* would see them.

We stopped at noon and Luke and I built a fire. We had *pashofa*, just like before. It was the best bowl of corn soup I'd ever had. I told my family about Joseph, and everything we'd seen and done.

"Where is Joseph?" Luke asked.

"He is waiting by the river. I should bring him a bowl of soup."

"Let me do it," Luke said. "I want to see him." Luke carried his blowgun in one hand and the bowl of *pashofa* in the other.

I wished Joseph could join us, but I knew it wasn't safe. When Luke returned, the bowl was empty.

"I gave him my blowgun," Luke said. "He's already making darts. I told him to take care of you. Joseph is a good friend."

"Maybe he can live with us when we reach our new home," my mother said. I held Jumper close to me and smiled. I knew my family would like Joseph. He was a strong Choctaw, one of us.

The day went by too fast. Soon the sky streaked red and the sun dipped below the hills. I knew it was time to go. I knew I would soon say that word again, and hear my family say it.

Chi pisa lachike.

Choctaws never say "good-bye." There is no word for it. We say "*chi pisa lachike,*" which means, "I will see you again, in the future." Even though I was nearing the day when I would never see my family as a living person, I would never leave them. Choctaws never go away.

Chapter 18

Trail of Tears

MY MOTHER HELD me for the longest time.

"*Chi pisa lachike*," she whispered. I think she knew.

But I didn't know. How could I? I had not seen a
ghost for days, it seemed. I thought they would at least
warn me. There was no warning.

We were halfway to the council wagon when Joseph
held up his hand. "Stop!" he said. "Did you hear that?"

I shook my head.

"There," he said, pointing to a small deer on the other
side of the river. He quietly slipped into the water, hold-
ing his blowgun high.

"Don't wait for me," he said over his shoulder. "I'm
going hunting."

I watched as Joseph climbed from the river and then

disappeared into the woods. I took a few steps, circled a fat tree trunk, and froze in my tracks. I knew something was wrong. I heard leaves flutter above me, and when I looked up, the wolf pounced.

He was so big. He knocked me to the ground and jumped on top of me. I tried to fight him off. I grabbed him and shook my head back and forth, so he couldn't bite my face.

I felt a sharp cutting pain. He sank his teeth into my neck. The wolf growled and threw his head back. His fangs dripped with blood.

My blood.

Soon the pain was gone. I closed my eyes. My body shivered and floated in a warm cloud. When I opened them, I was surrounded by so many Choctaws. Every Choctaw I had ever known who had died. They all were there.

The men and women sang the Choctaw friendship song, a song to welcome me. Young Choctaws waved at me. Each one held something, a blowgun, a boat paddle, a stickball bat, a cane fishing pole.

They wanted me to know that we were still Choctaws, always Choctaws, and that games and hunting and fishing still happen, even in the world of Choctaw ghosts.

I felt no ground beneath my feet. I felt lighter than air. I took a step to join the young ones.

"Noooo!" A scream pierced the cloud. I was alone again, back in the world of the living.

Joseph threw the deer to the ground and ran to help me. It was too late, but he didn't know. The wolf was carrying my body in his teeth. Joseph ran at him, left his feet, and sailed through the air. Before he struck the wolf, he was the panther.

I stood in my ghost body and watched them fight. The panther tore into the wolf, slashing him with his claws. The wolf dropped my body and fled into the woods.

The panther crouched beside me. He lowered his head and licked the blood from my face. As I watched, the black coat of the panther went away, like dark grass fading into the ground. I saw patches of skin, Joseph's skin, until finally it was only him, staring at my blood-covered body.

"No, no, no," he cried, over and over. "Why did you have to go? Not now. We have so much to do. You are my friend, my only friend, and I need you."

I felt helpless. I hated seeing Joseph so sad. I closed my eyes and felt the warm shiver. When I opened them, Old Man stood before me.

"You need to let him know," he said. "Joseph needs to see you."

"How can I do that?" I asked.

Old Man said nothing. He smiled and took me by the hand. Old Woman appeared beside him. They led me to Joseph.

"Speak to him," Old Man said, "and he will see you."

"Joseph," I whispered. My voice sounded like it always did. "I am still here."

Joseph turned his face to me.

"I am sorry," he said. "I should never have left you. I wish I had never seen that deer."

"Joseph, we both knew this was going to happen," I said. "Now that it's over, we can get to work. Naomi needs us."

"*Hoke*," he said. "But this will take some getting used to. I've never seen a ghost before."

"Just think of me like I think about you," I said. "I know you're there, even though I can't always see you."

"I can do that," Joseph said. "But promise me this. If you have to go away, let me know. I don't want the soldiers to capture me, tie me to a tree, and I'm not worried because I know you'll cut me loose, but you can't because you're off in the land of Choctaw ghosts! Can you promise me that won't happen?"

"I promise," I said.

Joseph was trying his best not to cry.

"Isaac, I have to tell your parents that you are dead," he said. "They have to take care of your body."

"This will not be easy." I was thinking of my mother. I followed Joseph back to my family. The snow had melted and the sun shone bright overhead. My family walked in the lead, and right behind them came Gabe and Ruth. Gabe held Nita's body, wrapped in her blanket.

Joseph stepped ten feet in front of them. When my mother saw him, she grabbed my father's arm and pulled him close.

"What is it?" my father asked. "Where is Isaac?"

Joseph hung his head. I could see he still blamed himself. My mother started crying, a soft muffled cry that turned the blue and sunny day into one of quiet mourning.

"What happened?" Luke asked.

"A wolf," Joseph said. He raised his head and looked at my father. "I am sorry. I fought the wolf but I wasn't quick enough. Isaac is gone."

My father pulled both families together and they sat beneath an old pine tree. He wrapped his arms around my mother and Luke and whispered a Choctaw prayer. They all cried, even Luke.

The passing walkers heard my family's sobs. They slowed down, bowed their heads, and said not a word, out of respect for the grieving family.

My father finally stood and threw a blanket over his shoulder. "Joseph, take us to his body," he said.

For the first time I realized what a burden I would be for my family. They would never leave my body behind, for animals to fight over my bones. Choctaws never leave their family's bones behind.

"I am going, too," said my mother.

No, please, I thought. I did not want my mother to see what the wolf had done to me.

As they neared the river, my father wrapped his arm around her and they walked so slowly, like a holy parade. Every step drew them closer to a sight they had hoped to never see.

Joseph circled my body and stood facing my parents. He didn't point or say a word. He bowed his head and looked at me, the face and chest and arms that used to be me. My eyes stared at the sky. The blood was dark red and covered the ground around me.

I felt a strong urge to end this grieving sadness. I wanted to leap into my body, to smile at them, to wipe away the blood and lift my arms. I wanted to stand up and let them know I was *hoke*.

Yes! I can do this, I thought. *I can float into my body and be with them again.* Then I remembered my father's words:

"You cannot keep your eyes on the bloody footprints you have left behind you. You must keep your eyes on where you are going."

I took a deep breath and watched.

My mother took the blanket from my father and laid it on the ground, away from the puddle of blood. My father rolled my body inside the blanket, wrapped his arms around me, and lifted me over his shoulder.

As Joseph waited in the woods, alone, they returned to the road and began their saddest day yet, carrying my body and walking on the Trail of Tears.

Chapter 19

Naomi Meets the Ghost

MY FATHER IS a hunter. So is my brother, Luke. They know the tracks of every animal and beast in the woods and swamps. As they left the woods with my body, I saw Luke tap my father on the shoulder and point to the ground. My father nodded.

They both saw the panther tracks, mixed with those of the wolf. Joseph's secret was no longer a secret to my family. They knew Joseph was the panther.

While my family began their slow walk, Joseph and I returned to the Choctaw Council wagon. At nightfall, while the others finished their meal, Nani Humma ambled to the river. He was looking for us.

"I'm over here," Joseph said, from his hiding spot in the bushes.

"Where is our friend?" Nani Humma asked.

"Isaac is dead," Joseph said. "A wolf attacked him. His family is carrying his body."

"Oh, Joseph," Nani Humma moaned. "Will the suffering ever be over?"

"Before you tell the others, know this," Joseph said. "Isaac always knew he would never reach our new home alive. He knew he would become a ghost. Now that it has happened, he is not afraid. His pain is over. He is with us now, and will stay with us till we rescue Naomi."

"You are a brave young man," Nani Humma said.

When we were alone again, Joseph lifted his palms, and asked, "Are you with me?"

"Yes," I assured him, and floated into view.

"No reason to wait. Let's go," he said.

The river curved way from the road. We left the riverbank and entered a thicket of oak trees. Joseph crept quietly, till we saw the flickering light of the soldiers' campfire.

"She's in the middle wagon," Joseph said.

Easier to keep an eye on her there, I thought.

"Isaac," he said, "the soldiers would see me before I reached her wagon, or they'd catch me when she cried out. She doesn't know me."

"She doesn't know me either," I said. But I knew what he was thinking.

"No," Joseph said, "but you can climb into the wagon without being seen. And you can whisper so soft, she'll listen to you. No Choctaw would scream to drive a ghost away, you know that. This is a job for you."

I knew he was right. "*Hoke*," I said. "But stay close!"

"I'll be right here, but what are you worried about?"

He was right. *What did I have to worry about?* That's when I realized, for the first time, that the soldiers couldn't hurt me. I was already dead! Maybe being a ghost wasn't so bad after all.

With my newfound courage, I walked to the soldiers' campfire. I sat down next to the man who had passed out the smallpox blankets. He could not see me, of course.

A young man was scooping beef stew from a large kettle and filling their bowls. He was Luke's age, more or less, but his arms were long and thin. His black hair was cut short, and I could see he was Choctaw.

Where is Naomi? I asked myself. *I thought she was their helper.*

Dumb me! Of course, this was Naomi, dressed like a teenage boy, with short-cut hair. *I have to be smarter than this*, I told myself.

"Hey, don't be so stingy," shouted a skinny soldier with a long pointy nose. "Gimme more stew! And where's the bread?"

Naomi took his bowl and refilled it. She hurried to the breadbasket and then handed over thick chunks of cornbread to every soldier.

"That's better," said Pointy Nose.

I waited and watched. The steam rose from the stewpot, but I couldn't smell a thing. Once Naomi tripped and splashed stew on my face. I jumped, out of habit. But I didn't feel anything, no blistery, burning skin.

When supper was over, the lead soldier stood up. He had curly black hair and a thick chest. I knew he would be a tough man to beat in a fight. He also had a serious look on his face.

"All right, we have another long day tomorrow," he said. "Let's get to bed." The others finished off their remaining stew and unrolled their blankets. I saw that some slept in the wagons; others, on the ground by the fire.

Those must be the guards, I thought.

"Who's got first watch?" Leader asked.

"Not me," said Pointy Nose.

"I'll take it," said a short, round soldier.

The other guards took off their boots and slipped under their blankets. Roundman rolled a log by the fire and sat down. His shotgun lay across his lap.

Moving among the soldiers should be easy, I knew that. But I also knew I had to be careful. If I knocked anything over or made too much noise, they would look for somebody sneaking around their camp.

I knew these men wouldn't care if they shot the right man or not. The closest Choctaw to their camp might end up dead because of me. It might be Nani Humma, wandering by the river at night.

I couldn't live with myself if that happened.

Naomi gathered the dirty bowls and stood by the campfire. The logs burned low and embers sparkled in the dark night air. I heard frogs calling from the river. Pointy Nose brought her a bucket of water, and Naomi washed the bowls.

"Let's go," Leader said to Naomi. She followed him to the middle covered wagon, and they climbed aboard.

He's tying her up with a rope, I thought.

I decided not to wait. When everyone was sleeping, any noise would alert the guards. Now was the time.

I tiptoed to the middle wagon. The wagon bed was high off the ground. Normally, I would have grabbed the rear board and swung my legs onto the wagon bed. But that would make too much noise.

I slid one arm over the rear board and scooted on my belly like a snake, trying to lift myself on the wagon. I fell through the wagon bed and hit the ground below!

I jumped to my feet and got ready to run.

Nobody moved. Nobody had heard me.

I tried to climb on the wagon again, but I kept falling to the ground.

"Isaac," Mister Jonah said, and he was laughing. "You need to remember, you are a ghost. You can't grab or move anything. You can't knock anything over; don't worry about that."

"How can I get inside the wagon then?" I asked. *Being a ghost was not so easy after all.*

"It's easier than you think," he said. "Just imagine where you want to be, and you're there."

"Do I close my eyes, like before?"

"You can if you want to," he said, still laughing, "but nobody else does."

"*Hoke*," I said, "I am inside the wagon." And I was! Mister Jonah was gone, and I floated above Naomi.

95

She lay curled up in a corner; her feet and hands tied to a thick nail. The ropes that bound her were short, forcing her to lie in the same spot. If she grew sore, she couldn't roll over, like everybody else does when they sleep.

I hovered above her and watched for a long moment. Her face was buried in her hands and she was crying.

"Naomi," I finally whispered.

"What took you so long?" she said.

Chapter 20

Naomi the Strong

"WHAT TOOK ME so long!" I said, far too loud. I clamped my hands over my mouth and listened. Nobody had heard me. Nobody *could* hear me.

"*Hoke*," I whispered. "What do you mean, 'What took me so long?' Do you know who I am?"

"No," Naomi said. "I do not know who you are. But I have been dreaming about you for a week. Every night you climb into my wagon. You are here to help me escape. But I cannot go with you."

I let her see me.

"Oooh," she said. Her voice was filled with wonder. "You are a ghost. I didn't know you would be a ghost."

"I have only been a ghost since this evening," I told her. "A wolf killed me, but I'm *hoke* now. Don't worry about me. We need to get you home to your family. We've been planning your escape for several days."

"Is that why the Choctaw councilwomen come by?"

"Yes. You see everything, don't you?" I said.

"I have to be watchful to stay alive," Naomi said. "But you must understand. I can't leave or the soldiers will take my little sister."

"I know Nita," I said. "And I know your family. They walk with mine."

"How are they?" Naomi asked.

"They are sad, Naomi. Nita is gone. She died four days ago."

Naomi shook her head. "No," she said. Fat balls of tears rolled down her cheeks. "Not my little sister. How did she die?"

"She rolled out of her blanket and froze to death," I said. "Nita is my little sister, too. She adopted me."

Naomi shook with sadness, and I waited for her to finish crying. Grieving is hard. Lives are changed forever by grieving.

"The soldiers can't hurt her anymore," she sobbed. "They already killed her." After a long time, she wiped the tears from her eyes and asked, "Can you talk to her?"

"Yes," I said. "It was Nita's idea that we bring you home. She said you would make your family happy again. That's why I am here, Naomi."

I should have known Nita would follow me. But I was as surprised as Naomi when I heard her voice.

"Naomi," Nita giggled. "Give me a big hug." Nita

shone like a pale moon. I could see through her. But there she was, wrapping her ghost arms around her big sister, Naomi.

"Nita," Naomi said. "I am so happy to see you!"

"See," Nita said. "You can make Mommy and Daddy happy, too."

I wanted to talk to Naomi about an escape plan. But that never happened, not on this night.

"Naomi!" A voice shouted from the rear of the wagon. Leader waved a bright lantern from one corner of the wagon to the other.

"Who's in there with you? I heard voices."

"No one," Naomi said, trembling. "I was having a nightmare. I must have been talking in my sleep. I am sorry I woke you."

Leader held the lantern close to the ground and circled the wagon.

He is looking for tracks, I thought. *I hope ghosts don't leave footprints.*

"Who were you talking to?" Leader hollered, louder than before.

"No one," Naomi said. "I was asleep."

He knew she was lying. He climbed into the wagon and untied her hands and feet. With one strong arm he lifted her and tossed her to the ground.

I jumped to her side and tried to drag her away. My hands passed through her. I could do nothing to help her.

This was all my fault.

I wanted to run to the river for Joseph, but I was afraid

to leave Naomi. Leader was so mad. I feared he would hurt her.

"Don't move!" Leader shouted. He took a rope from the wagon and tossed it over a strong tree limb. I froze at the horror of what I was watching.

No, please no. He is going to hang her! I thought.

Leader grabbed Naomi by the waist. The other soldiers stood watching. They knew better than to say a word, but I could tell what they were thinking. It was written on their faces: *When Leader is this mad, he'll strike anyone or anything in his way.* They stared without moving as Leader dragged Naomi to the rope, dangling on the ground beneath the tree.

"Give me your hands!" he said.

Naomi lifted her hands, and he tied the rope tight around her wrists. "I need some help!" he yelled.

Roundman and Pointy Noise ran to his side.

"Take this rope and pull it till I say stop," he ordered.

They tugged on the rope and Naomi rose to her feet, lifted by the rope tied to her wrists. She clenched her jaw tight shut. I saw by the wild look in her eyes that Naomi was afraid for her life.

They pulled on the rope till Naomi was standing, her arms high over her head.

"Keep pulling!" Leader shouted. "I didn't say stop!"

Pointy Nose and Round man yanked hard on the rope.

"Ohhhh!" Naomi screamed. Leader slapped her hard across the face.

"You will never lie to me again," he said. He moved

his face so close to hers, I could not hear what he was saying. It must have been horrible. Naomi closed her eyes
and shook her head back and forth.

When Naomi's feet were at his waist, Leader turned
back to his helpers.

"Now, you can stop," he said. "Tie the rope to the tree
trunk." Naomi swung slowly, twisting and swaying. Her
face was etched in pain.

"Now," Leader said. "It's getting late. We have a long
day tomorrow. Men, let's get some sleep."

As if she were a dog tied to a stake, they left her. They
left my new friend Naomi hanging from a tree. I heard a
soft cry and knew without looking who it was.

"We did this to her. Didn't we?" Nita said.

"Yes, Nita, I think we did," I said. There was no reason
to lie. "But we will not leave her here."

We hurried to the river, where Joseph was waiting.

"Joseph," I said, "you have to see this." I led him to the
soldiers' campsite. By the light of the dying fire, Naomi
hung.

"We can't wait any longer," Joseph said. "Naomi comes
with us tonight."

Chapter 21

The Panther and the Fire

"DO YOU STILL HAVE your cutting stone?" I asked Joseph, as we hid behind the tree.

"Yes, always. I'll cut her down. I can slip up behind her, but once she's on her feet, the guards will come after us. And they don't have to outrun us. They have shotguns."

"I can lead her to her family," I said.

"We need some way to distract the soldiers," Joseph said, "some way to slow them down."

"I think a strong panther could handle the soldiers," I said. "You've done it before."

"What can I do?" Nita asked.

"You can wake up the Choctaw Council, the men and women, all of them. Let them know what happened. When the soldiers chase us, they can delay them.

Every minute is important," I said.

"I understand," Nita said. She disappeared into the night fog, a five-year-old Choctaw girl — a ghost — making her first appearance before the Choctaw Council. Her sister's life was at stake.

Joseph and I circled the camp. Pointy Nose and Roundman sat on a log by the fire, their shotguns close-by. We crept behind the tree and waited. The quarter moon cast a bright light through the naked branches of the tree.

Joseph pointed to the sky. A huge cloud moved across the sky. I understood. We would wait till the cloud covered the moon.

"You take first watch," said Pointy Nose. "I'm going to sleep."

"That's not a good idea," Roundman said. "You saw how mad he was. If something happens, we'll be hanging from that tree. And not by our wrists."

"He wouldn't hang us!" Pointy Nose said.

"Want to risk your life?" asked Roundman. "Not me. You stay here and I'll watch the girl." He rose and moved by the tree where Naomi hung. Roundman leaned against the trunk, three feet from us!

We sat so quiet, in fear for our lives. If Roundman stepped around the tree, all three of us would be dead. He held his shotgun ready to fire.

What happened next could never be planned.

Something licked me on the ankle. I looked at my feet. There stood Jumper, wagging his tail and ready to play! I froze.

Please don't let him bark, I thought. I wanted to ask him how he had found me, but there was no time. We needed a distraction, and Jumper was ready to play.

As quietly as I could, I ran to the river and Jumper dashed after me. At just the right moment, the cloud covered the moon and the sky turned dark. With a loud splash, Jumper dove in the river!

"What was that?" Roundman shouted.

"Something fell in the river," Pointy Nose said, and the two soldiers followed the noise.

Boom! Roundman's shotgun blasted and soon the camp was scrambling with soldiers.

"What's going on!" shouted Leader, as he hurried to the riverbank.

"Someone stay with the girl," said Leader, and a soldier stayed behind. He touched Naomi's feet with the barrel of his shotgun. Naomi jerked.

"Don't you worry," he said, with a cruel smile in his voice. "You're not going anywhere."

I hid behind the hanging tree. No one could see me, I was sure of that. Joseph was gone. I heard a clawing sound and looked above me. The panther crouched on the tree limb, gnawing on the rope.

Suddenly, Naomi fell to the ground. The panther leapt on the soldier and his shotgun went flying.

"We have to run," I said. "Can you make it?"

"Lead the way," she said. She was shaking, but I knew she was strong. Her wrists were still tied to the rope, but we had no time to stop. She dragged the rope behind her as she ran. The panther ran to the fire and slapped the burning logs, sending fiery embers all about the camp.

Boom! Boom! Boom! The soldiers fired at Jumper in the river.

"Let him be," shouted Leader. "It's only a dog."

"Look!" said Roundman. "The camp is on fire!"

The soldiers returned to camp, ready for battle. Panther Joseph was ready, too. He gripped a burning log in his teeth and jumped into a wagon. The cloth top of the wagon burst into flames.

The panther wasn't finished. He roared his panther cry and jumped under the burning wagon, hiding himself in the flames. When the wagon collapsed, he leapt to a tree, climbed up the trunk, and disappeared in the branches.

Two soldiers surrounded the tree and fired their shotguns overhead. A blast hit the limb where the panther crouched. Before it hit the ground, the panther jumped on the soldiers, knocking both of them off their feet.

With all eyes on the panther, Naomi and I were far from the camp before they realized she was gone. When we arrived at the Choctaw Council wagon everyone was wide-awake. They were expecting us.

Nita did her job, I thought.

"You are the captured girl?" a councilwoman asked.

"Yes," said Naomi.

"Here," she said, "let me help you." She hurried to the wagon and returned with a sharp knife. She sliced the rope and tossed it in the campfire.

"We don't want the soldiers to see that," she said.

105

"Now, you must leave. The soldiers will be here soon. Can you find your way to your family by yourself?"

"I am not by myself," Naomi said. I realized the woman couldn't see me. I floated into sight.

"Oh," the councilwoman said, "I see you are protected by our ghost friend. But you must hurry. We'll do what we can to stop them."

We ran without looking behind. I soon realized Naomi was faster than me. This was only my first day, I hadn't learned to run like a ghost!

The panther was faster than us both. The soldiers fired their guns at us, but we had a big lead. They returned to their camp and the burning wagon, while we hurried down the line of walkers, nearing my family's camp.

Luke saw us first. "You must be Naomi," he said. "We don't have time to talk, not now. You know you can't stay here. Your mother and father are with my family. This is the first place they will look."

My parents stood with Gabe and Ruth.

"Where can I go?" Naomi asked.

"We have a wagon ready," said Luke. "Follow me."

"Wait," Naomi said.

"There is no time," said Luke. "We have to go!"

"There is time for this," Naomi said. She stretched out her arms and her mother and father ran to greet her.

"We were so afraid for you," Ruth said.

"You know that Nita is gone?" asked Gabe.

"Hey!" Nita's sweet voice always came when least expected.

She floated into sight. "I'm not gone. I'm just a ghost, but I am still part of the family."

Only Nita could bring smiles on a day like today.

"Of course," said Ruth, "family stays together. Always."

"You better be going," Gabe said.

"*Chi pisa lachike*," they whispered. Both of my families waved when we left the camp.

"*Chi pisa lachike*," they said.

We followed Luke to a Choctaw wagon a half-mile down the road.

"They are waiting for you," he said. "We didn't know you would come so soon. But after Nita spoke to us, we told them everything. They are ready to hide you, Naomi."

Luke led us to the rear of the covered wagon.

Who would risk their lives by hiding Naomi? I asked myself.

I soon had my answer.

"We are here!" Luke called to the people in the wagon. An old woman with wrinkled skin and long white hair stuck her head through the curtain. She nodded and flung the curtain open. Three even older women smiled and welcomed Naomi into their wagon, into their world.

The world of the bonepickers.

I lifted my arms and passed through the wagon walls.

Chapter 22

Buried with the Bones

"WE HAVE BEEN waiting for you," said the woman. "Take your shoes off before you climb in the wagon. We keep everything neat and clean."

Naomi leaned against a wheel and slipped off her boots.

"Here," said the woman, "hand them to me. I'll hide them for you." She helped Naomi into the wagon and closed the flap. Once inside, Naomi was struck by the smell of dried rose petals.

"Mmmm," she said, "it smells nice in here." The women were silent, but Naomi thought she heard soft laughter.

"We are so used to the smells, we barely notice," said the woman. "But we try to keep everything nice for the others."

"What others?" asked Naomi.

More soft laughter floated from the rear of the wagon.

"Everybody else," said the woman. "Most people don't like to be around us."

"Why not?" The words had barely passed through Naomi's lips when she wished she had never uttered them. In a sudden flash, like a thunderbolt that shook her very being, Naomi realized where she was.

"I'm in the wagon of the bonepickers," she whispered.

Few Choctaws have ever seen the bonepickers, but everyone knew of them. Before the soldiers came, they lived in a thicket of trees, deep in the piney woods. They never left their tiny log house.

A small pond lay close to their back door, gushing warm water from far underground. A young man brought them food and supplies, so they never had to leave home. Their job was the hardest and most sacred in all of Choctaw country.

When a Choctaw died, the body was brought to the bonepickers. They carried the body to a wooden platform close to the spring, where animals came to drink. After days, sometimes weeks, when the wolves and buzzards had eaten the flesh from the bones, the bonepickers began their real task.

They carried the body inside and picked the bones clean. They washed and scrubbed the bones till they were shiny and white. With a thin rope made from the clothing, they tied the bones into a bundle. This bundle was now ready for burial.

This was the Choctaw way.

And now, with Choctaws forced to walk, the bonepickers had to leave their home, too. They were too old to walk. Urged by the Choctaw

109

Council, the soldiers gave them a wagon. This was the wagon Naomi had climbed into, a wagon sweetened by the smell of dried roses.

"Don't worry, dear child," the woman said. "Don't be afraid of us. This is the safest place for you now. If the soldiers search the wagon, we have a place for you."

Naomi's eyes adjusted to the darkness. She saw the three older women, curled together at the rear of the wagon. They surrounded a large wooden trunk.

"Here," said the woman, lifting the lid. "You will be safe in the trunk."

Naomi took a deep breath and froze. The trunk was filled with bones!

"Don't be afraid," the woman said. "You do not have to touch the bones. The men built a secret hiding place for you."

The woman piled the bones into two large sacks. While Naomi watched, they lifted the floor of the trunk.

"It has a secret bottom, a tiny place for you to lie and wait till the soldiers go away. Here, climb inside."

Naomi crawled into the trunk, lay on her back, and closed her eyes.

"Take this," said the woman, handing Naomi a blanket. "This will keep you warm."

The women settled the wooden plank on top of her, and emptied the bags of bones into the trunk.

Naomi heard the bones scatter and roll, only a few inches above her head. The air was stuffy, but she could breathe. She curled under the blanket and waited.

I hope I don't have to stay here long, she thought.

"I know what you're thinking," the woman said, and the bonepickers laughed. "We'll do our best to see that your stay is short."

"Oh, don't say that," said an older women, in a cracked and tiny voice. "She seems so nice. Maybe she can stay and help us."

Naomi felt the wagon move. The bones creaked and rattled above her. She listened while the woman spoke to Luke.

"Have your panther friend bring us a small animal from the woods, a possum or raccoon," she said.

"I'll tell him right away," said Luke.

"Tell him to gnaw the animal, make it good and bloody!" the woman shouted. "The more blood the better!"

Chapter 23

Naomi and the Bonepickers

I KNEW NAOMI needed me, now more than ever. I slipped through the walls of the trunk. I was learning when to disappear and when to be seen. I let my body give off a soft glow, slowly coming to life before her eyes.

"Do everything they say and you will be safe," I whispered. "Joseph will be nearby, to warn us when the soldiers come. They'll never find you here."

"Why do they want a bloody animal?" Naomi asked.

"I don't know. We'll have to wait and see."

We didn't have long to wait. After only a few minutes, Panther Joseph caught a fat raccoon. He dragged the dead raccoon across the ground, then crouched and leapt into the wagon, dropping the raccoon before the bonepickers.

I lifted my arms and floated through the top of the trunk. I wanted to see what the woman would do with a bloody dead raccoon. Panther Joseph had done what she asked. The raccoon was slashed and cut from head to tail.

Panther teeth cuts, I thought.

A thick trail of blood stretched across the floor of the wagon. The woman took the raccoon by the neck and flung it in a circle over her head. Blood flew everywhere, on the walls, the trunk, and all over the woman. She lifted the lid of the trunk and held the raccoon over the pile of bones.

As I watched, the woman squeezed the raccoon tight and wrung it out, like she was squeezing water from a wet towel.

Blood dripped on the bones.

"Oh!" Naomi shouted.

I returned to the trunk and hovered over Naomi.

"I'm here, Naomi," I said.

"Help me," Naomi whispered.

Blood dripped through the cracks in the floor and fell like raindrops on Naomi's face.

"Nooo," she cried.

"Shhhh," said the woman. "We have to do this. Once the soldiers look in the trunk, they'll leave us alone."

"She's right, Naomi," I whispered. "Nothing scares *Nahullos* like bloody bones."

"I think I'd rather be a ghost," said Naomi.

"Don't think like that. What about your mother and father? One ghost daughter is enough."

"You're right," she said. "*Hoke*, just get me out of here as soon as you can."

"I'll do my best, but I have to leave you now."

Luke and Joseph waited for me by the river. The snow fell thick and they were shivering cold. Bits of blood and raccoon fur dotted Joseph's face and hair.

"You should wash up before anybody sees you," I told him.

"Oh, sorry," said Joseph. He grabbed a handful of snow and washed himself clean.

"How long will Naomi stay with the bonepickers?" he asked.

"Till it's safe," Luke answered. "Remember they are looking for a girl with short hair, cut like a boy's. The women have a plan to hide Naomi in plain sight. They are weaving a long hairpiece for her to wear."

"It might work," said Joseph. "For now, Isaac and I will wait here. We'll let you know when anything happens," Joseph said.

"I'll do the same," Luke promised. "I need to get back to the family. *Chi pisa lachike*."

"Don't go yet," a deep voice said.

Luke stopped in his tracks. He stood speechless, his eyes filled with wonder. A thick white cloud covered us, and when it lifted, Old Man stood among us.

I am the only ghost Luke has ever seen, I thought. *He's entering my world now, the living place of ghosts.*

"We want to tell you three young men how proud we

114

are of what you have done today," Old Man said.

He nodded and lifted his arms. In the dark of the woods the air trembled with light. One by one they appeared, until at least a hundred Choctaw ghosts encircled us.

They were the walking ones who never left us. In times of trouble they are there. We know this, but sometimes we must be reminded.

Our deeds touch not only the living. We did more than save Naomi today. We made our people proud. That is the highest honor a Choctaw can ever earn, to make the ancestors proud.

They spoke in a single voice and with a single word they honored us.

"*Yakoke*," they said. "Thank you."

As suddenly as they appeared, the ghosts were gone. Luke said not a word. He looked at Joseph and me, then turned quickly and started home. When he thought we weren't looking, he broke into a run.

"He'll get used to it," said Joseph.

"He'd better," I said, "now that his little brother is a ghost."

Sometime after midnight the wind grew angry and sleet replaced the friendly snow. Watching the ice fall, I was glad to be a ghost. I couldn't feel a thing. Joseph wrapped himself tight in my blanket, but I knew he was freezing. We couldn't risk a fire.

"The snow has covered our footprints," I said, "and the ice will slow them down in the morning."

"Yes, I'm glad for that," Joseph said, through chattering teeth. "Let's hope for more ice!"

As if in reply, a branch heavy with ice cracked and landed at our feet.

"Careful what you wish for," I reminded him.

Chapter 24

A Soldier's Vow

IN SPITE OF THE FREEZING cold, Joseph fell asleep in minutes. His blanket was soon covered in snow. I knew he was exhausted from the long day of rescuing Naomi, setting fire to the soldiers' camp, rushing Naomi to the bonepickers' wagon, and catching a raccoon with his bare teeth!

I sat watching him sleep. I was neither tired nor cold.

Life is very different as a ghost, I told myself. I learned something else that night: Without sleep, life as a ghost can be boring!

That must be why ghosts know everything, I thought. *While everybody else is sleeping, they float around and see what's happening.*

I closed my eyes tight and imagined the soldiers' camp.

When I opened them, I stood by the burning wagon. The soldiers had tried to put the fire out with buckets of snow, but the wagon was destroyed. Piles of smoking embers were all that remained.

Roundman leaned against a tree, wide-awake, with his shotgun over his lap. The other soldiers were asleep in their wagons. I searched the wagons till I found Leader. He was tossing and turning, adrift in a nightmare of the fire and Naomi's escape.

"I will kill you for this!" he called out in his sleep.

His anger was strong, and I knew he would seek revenge in the morning. I returned to my family's camp. Everyone was safe and sound asleep. Nita lay between her mother and father. She smiled and waved at me.

"Where have you been?" Jumper asked.

"Jumper," I said, "I've missed you!"

"Yeah, life's not the same without you, either."

"Is everything *hoke*?" I asked.

"*Hoke* for now, but stay close in the morning. Trouble's coming. That's what everybody says."

"Well, everybody is right. The soldiers will be looking for you, you know."

"How'd you like my little act?" Jumper said with pride. "I jumped in the river and got their attention, so you and Joseph could save Naomi. That water was cold, but it was worth it."

"You were great, Jumper! But this battle is not over quite yet," I said. "Get some sleep, and I'll see you in the morning."

"*Chi pisa lachike*," Jumper said. When he saw the surprised look on my face, he added, "What? You never heard a dog speak Choctaw before?"

"Jumper, you have to be the smartest dog in the world!"

"*Yakoke*," said Jumper.

I waved good-bye as I floated away.

The light of day came slow and quiet that morning. No red streaks in the sky announced the sunrise. I circled the soldiers' camp till one by one they rolled out of bed and joined Leader by the campfire.

"Stay together today," Leader said. "We will find the girl. She and her family will pay. Feed the horses well and carry extra shotgun shells. If anyone runs, shoot them."

"Do you want anyone to guard the camp?" asked Pointy Nose.

"No!" shouted Leader. He grabbed his shotgun and walked slowly to Pointy Nose. "Ask me that again," he said, in a low and menacing voice.

"Do . . . you want anyone . . . to guard the camp?" Pointy Nose stammered.

Leader tilted his hat to the back of his head and looked to the sky. Every soldier stared at him, unsure of what he would do next. Leader took a step back, lifted his shotgun to his shoulder, and swung it hard at the skinny soldier.

Pointy Nose fell to the ground, with blood flowing from a cut on his forehead.

"Do you have your answer?" Leader shouted. "No guards! You are not getting out of this!"

Roundman leapt to his friend and wrapped a cloth around his head. Blood soaked through the cloth, and Roundman packed the wound with snow to stop the bleeding.

"Now," said Leader, "saddle your horses and let's go. We will search every wagon, starting with the Choctaw Council's. Climb in the wagons and search in every corner. When you find the girl, bring her to me."

As the soldiers mounted their horses and stepped to the icy road, Leader shouted, "Someone will die today."

Chapter 25

A Day of Death

TWENTY SOLDIERS ON horseback rode behind Leader. As they approached the camp of the Choctaw Council, he held his hand high. The soldiers waited. Joseph crouched beside me, watching from the shadows.

"Shotguns!" Leader shouted. The soldiers lifted their guns to their shoulders.

"You are welcome in our camp," said Mister Tibbi. He rose from the campfire and stepped to the soldiers, who held their guns ready to fire.

"Take aim!" shouted Leader. He pointed to the tree limbs hanging over the council members, men and women both.

"Let us talk about what happened last night," said Mister Tibbi. Leader ignored the Choctaw councilman, as if he were nothing more than a patch of snow on the road.

"Fire!" shouted Leader.

Boom! Boom! Boom! Twenty shotguns exploded, shattering the treetops. Ice-covered branches fell all about the camp, destroying the fire circle and toppling the cooking pot. A large tree limb ripped through the roof of the wagon. Joseph quickly turned into the panther and growled with anger.

"Joseph, no," I shouted. "The soldiers will shoot you. You can't escape twenty men in daylight. Stop, please. Naomi needs you alive."

The panther turned to look at me.

"After you burned the wagon last night," I said, "they would love to parade your body for everyone to see. You don't want that. Naomi could die, too." The panther paused at the mention of Naomi. His dark coat receded, and soon Joseph knelt beside me.

At first glance, the Choctaw council members appeared to be safe, but soon a low moan rose from beneath a heavy branch.

"Stella," a woman shouted. "Help me, someone!"

Two councilmen rolled the limb away, and elderly Stella lay unconscious. A large purple bruise covered one cheek and her eye was swollen shut.

Mister Tibbi stood his ground.

"We did nothing to deserve this," he said, in a quiet but strong voice. Leader leaned from his saddle and, for the first time, spoke to Mister Tibbi.

"You are lucky no one died," he said. "But the day is

not over yet. Find the girl and bring her to us."

Mister Tibbi turned to his camp. Nani Humma dragged the tree limb from the wagon and the women circled fallen Stella.

"Let's move!" shouted Leader. The soldiers tugged the reins and moved their horses down the road.

As Joseph and I watched, something changed among the uniformed horsemen, some new cloud of fear hung in the air. Since they had left their campsite, only a short while ago, they had become deeply afraid of Leader. They had stood and stared, helpless to stop him, as he struck Pointy Nose with his shotgun.

He might have killed him, they realized. Privately they wondered, *What might he do to me?*

But seeing how helpless the Choctaw council members had been, with no guns or weapons, the soldiers also felt a new power, the power of life and death. They reloaded their shotguns as they rode, eager for the day. By the time they reached the next camp, their fear had turned to anger.

"No walking!" Leader shouted at the next group of Choctaws, sitting quietly around their morning fire. "You," he said, pointing to a young Choctaw man. "Run to the others and tell them to stay where they are. No walking today."

He turned to his waiting soldiers. "Turn the camp inside out. Burn the blankets," he said.

The soldiers leapt from their horses and invaded the camp. They tore blankets from women and children huddled from the cold. They threw the blankets into the fire. If a man stood in their way, they knocked him to the ground.

Word soon spread up and down the line of Choctaw walkers.

"The soldiers are coming!"

When the soldiers arrived at every camp, they found Choctaws standing away from the fires, clinging to their children. As they rode from the camps, flames lifted high from the burning blankets. Curls of smoke filled the air, as closer and closer the soldiers came to my family.

"Joseph, I have to warn them," I said. "They'll come after Naomi's parents. I'm going." In a moment I stood by the campfire where my two families gathered. I closed my eyes and came to life before their eyes.

"Are we safe?" my father asked.

"Yes," I said. "Let them have your blankets and say nothing."

"They are looking for Naomi, aren't they?" Gabe asked.

"Yes, and they are angry," I said. "They don't know Nita is dead. They'll be looking to take her."

"What should we do?"

"Show them her body," I said. "Unroll the blanket and let them see that she is dead."

"I do not want the soldiers to cast their eyes on my little girl," Ruth sobbed. "They might take her body from us; they might try to burn it."

"Mother," said the tiny voice we had come to expect. Nita appeared. "I am here. I am with you. My body is not me. Whatever the soldiers do, let them do."

"Nita is right," I said. "When the sun sets on this day, we want everyone to be safe. If they scatter Nita's bones, we will gather them. If they burn her bones, we will gather the ashes. We are Choctaws. We are stronger than the soldiers."

I could not believe I had spoken those words.

For a long moment, everyone stared at me in silence. A warm yellow cloud rose from the fire and filled the air. Old Man appeared in the cloud. Soon he was joined by every Choctaw from our town, the living and the dead. Our tiny camp was filled with hundreds of people.

The living people looked confused, not knowing where they were or how they came to be here.

Finally, Old Man spoke.

"The young man is right," he said, nodding to me. "Every Choctaw needs to hear his words."

Though my lips didn't move, my voice filled the air, and I heard myself say once more, "When the sun sets on this day, we want everyone to be safe. If they scatter Nita's bones, we will gather them. If they burn her bones, we will gather the ashes.

"We are Choctaws. We are stronger than the soldiers."

Chapter 26

Choctaw Rattlesnake

"THERE THEY ARE!" Leader shouted. "The girl's family! They know where she is." The soldiers circled the camp, staying on their horses.

"My daughter isn't here," said Gabe, stepping forward. "We do not know where she is. Search all you like, you will not find her here."

"She can't be far," Leader said, turning to the soldiers. "If she tries to run, don't shoot her. She needs to suffer for the trouble she's caused."

"What about you?" Leader said, pointing to my father. "Have you seen a girl with short hair, dressed like a boy?"

"I do not know where she is," my father replied.

"Then I must believe you," said Leader. His voice was evil and his face was hard. "What reason would you have to lie? I guess you've heard by now, this girl has escaped. But we don't need to find her. We have a promise to keep."

He turned to Gabe. "Where is your other daughter, the little one?"

"She is no longer with us," Gabe said.

"You are lying!" Leader hissed. "Bring her to me now!"

I expected Ruth to cry, but she did not. Instead, she carried Nita's body, wrapped in the blanket, and laid it by the fire.

"Here is my daughter," she said, and unrolled the blanket. Nita looked so small and helpless. Her face was swollen and her eyes were shut tight.

The soldiers stepped back and looked away. I felt the warm shiver creep through my skin. I closed my eyes and hoped. I did not want to see how anyone would die, not today.

When I opened my eyes, I saw children hovering close to their fathers. Boys and girls clung to their soldier fathers. Many were the same age as Nita, whose body now lay before them.

The soldiers have children, I thought, *and they are hoping this never happens to any of them.* Thinking of their children, the soldiers hung their heads and waited for their orders.

"What would you like us to do?" Pointy Nose asked. I knew by his manner that he had no children. Nita's death meant nothing to him. He was more concerned with winning back Leader's trust.

"Well," said Leader, "I am glad to see that one of us

is not afraid of death. Roll her up and take her with us!"

"Be glad to," Pointy Nose replied, with a thin smirk on his face. He stooped to Nita's body.

I saw Gabe look at my father. My father nodded, so slightly the soldiers didn't see.

They share a secret, I thought. *What do they know?*

Pointy Nose reached for the blanket, but something stopped him. His eyes grew large and a look of fear replaced the smirk. A soft sound filled the silence, a soft whirring sound. It grew louder and louder till the air around us shook with the sound.

Whirrrr! Whirrrr! Whirrrr!

The head of a rattlesnake weaved back and forth over Nita's body.

"Sir," said Pointy Nose, "I can . . . not . . . please don't make me do this."

"Shut up!" Leader said. "Get back on your horse. We can't waste our time here."

He turned to Gabe and Ruth.

"You have lost one daughter already," Leader said, "so I cannot keep my promise. But I made a vow this morning. Someone will die today. We will find the girl and she will die."

As the soldiers rode away, the snake lowered his head and coiled into a tight circle. Ruth looked at Gabe and my father, then knelt to Nita's body.

"*Yakoke*," she whispered. She bowed her head over her daughter, and the snake disappeared in a thin cloud of curling smoke.

Only later would I learn who cast the spell and brought the snake. On this morning I simply bowed my head like everyone else and whispered my gratitude.

"*Yakoke.*"

Chapter 27

Wagon of the Bonepickers

THE SOLDIERS CONTINUED their search, burning blankets and questioning Choctaws at every camp. By noon they arrived at the wagon of the bonepickers, the final stop.

I stepped through the walls of the trunk to warn Naomi. "They are here," I whispered.

"Did they hurt my family?" she asked.

"No, your family is safe, but Leader is furious. He wants to hurt you. Whatever happens, don't make a sound."

"I am ready for this day to be over," she said. "My body is stiff from lying here so long."

"You won't have long to wait," I said. The words had barely left my lips when the soldiers stormed into camp. I waited for Leader to bark his orders. I heard the horses shuffling around the wagon, but Leader was silent. I lifted myself from the trunk and floated through the wagon.

Leader waved his arms and motioned for the soldiers to dismount. The bonepickers huddled together in the wagon.

"Where is everyone?" Roundman asked.

Leader stared hard at him, moving his finger to his lips for silence. He stepped to the wagon and flung the curtain aside.

"Come out, now!" he yelled.

No one moved.

"Get out of the wagon!"

The bonepickers, one by one, climbed from the wagon. They were old and moved so slowly, stepping down with feeble, unsure legs. Leader grew impatient.

"Move!" he shouted. The oldest bonepicker was the last to leave. Her legs were so short her feet dangled in the air, searching a safe place to step. Leader grabbed her by the arm and threw her to the ground. A soldier moved to help her.

"Leave her alone," Leader said. His chest was heaving back and forth. "Someone will die today," he said in a mean, low voice, staring hard at the soldier. "It might be you."

The soldiers froze. They looked at the old woman lying at their feet. I felt the warm shiver washing over me and closed my eyes. When I opened them, I was surrounded by dozens of older *Nahullo* women.

They are spirit people, I thought. *Ghosts. They are the*

131

grandmothers, the mothers, and aunts of the soldiers.

The women wrapped their arms around the soldiers, and though their arms floated through the air, touching nothing, they smiled and talked among themselves. They were overjoyed to see their young men.

The soldiers could not see the ghost women, but their memories were strong. I could see it in their faces. They winced as they stared at the fallen bonepicker.

What if that was my mother? they seemed to be thinking. They looked at Leader, and saw for the first time the cruel man they were bound by law to follow.

Leader shouted at the bonepickers standing before him.

"Where is she? You are hiding the girl, I know it. Speak to me!"

The bonepickers moved to help their fallen friend. *They are frail but they are brave,* I thought.

"Leave her alone!" Leader yelled.

The bonepickers ignored him and he grew madder still.

"Drag everything from the wagon," he said. Two soldiers stepped forward and entered the wagon. I floated in beside them.

"There is blood everywhere," a soldier said. "Nothing here but an old trunk."

"Open it," Leader said, leaning inside the wagon. The soldier lifted the lid and stepped back in horror.

"The trunk is full of bones," the soldier said. "They are covered in blood."

Leader turned to the bonepickers.

"What are you hiding?" The bonepickers huddled together and spoke not a word. Nothing Leader did or said meant anything to them.

"I don't think they understand English," said Roundman.

"Maybe they will understand this," Leader replied. He stepped to the campfire, picked up a burning log, and handed it to Roundman.

"Burn the wagon," he said in a quiet voice.

No! I thought. *Naomi is still inside.*

"Please help her," Nita whispered in my ear. I entered the wagon and tried to lift the lid, but my hands passed through the trunk. Roundman tossed the burning log in the wagon. The dry wood and cloth caught fire and the wagon burst into flames.

From his hiding place in the cedar trees, Joseph saw everything. He leapt from a low hanging branch and landed near the wagon.

"Grab him!" Leader shouted. A soldier tackled Joseph and wrestled him to the ground.

"Well," said Leader, "we thought the panther killed you."

Joseph said nothing. Flames shot into the sky, and soon the wagon was a tower of fire. Scorching heat cracked the air. The soldiers covered their faces and stepped back. Joseph relaxed and the soldier loosened his grip, just enough.

Joseph wiggled free and dashed to the wagon. He leapt through the burning curtain as the soldier grabbed his legs.

"Let him go," said Leader. "My prophecy comes true. Let him burn."

Nita and I entered the smoke-filled wagon. Flames crept up the walls of the trunk. Joseph flung open the lid and tossed the bones aside. He lifted the false floor and pulled Naomi to her feet. She was covered in blood and looked more dead than alive.

"We are here for you," Joseph said. Naomi shook with fear, but her face looked strong. Somehow I knew she would live through this day.

"They are watching the rear of the wagon," Joseph yelled, over the sound of the crackling flames. "We'll jump through the cloth wall."

He ripped a piece of burning wood from the floor and held it to the cloth. The flames ignited and they waited for the circle of fire to grow. Naomi slapped embers from her hair and clothes.

"They are waiting too long," I said. "They will burn to death."

"No," said Nita. "They know what they're doing."

As the roof of the wagon collapsed in a mound of flames, Joseph took Naomi by the hand and they jumped from the wagon. By the time they were spotted, they were almost to the river.

"After them!" Leader yelled, but his voice was drowned out by the sound of the wagon crashing. All eyes remained on the burning wagon — and the bonepickers huddled together quietly and unafraid of death.

While the soldiers watched, the women kicked aside

the still burning boards, searching for any remaining bones.

Leader jumped on his horse and rode after Joseph and Naomi. They dashed to the river, with Leader close behind. It looked like he would catch them, but his horse slipped on a rock overhang and Leader jerked the reins. His horse bucked and sent Leader flying from the saddle.

His head struck hard against the rock. Blood gushed from a gash on his forehead, but he scrambled to his feet.

"They're safe for now, Nita," I said. I knew they could outrun him. Leader was staggering. He grabbed a tree trunk to steady himself.

Suddenly, Naomi stopped.

"Run," said Joseph. "Follow me. I know a place to hide."

Naomi shook her head and pointed to a dark cavern beneath the rock. I followed her gaze and froze in terror at what I saw. I closed my eyes, hoping this was all a ghost vision, a terrible vision that would go away.

Please, don't let this happen, I thought.

Chapter 28

Panther and the Wolf

WHEN I OPENED my eyes, the wolf that had killed me was crawling from the cavern. He lowered his head and stared at Naomi, then slowly turned his head to look at Joseph. He bared his teeth and growled a low growl. He lifted his head and sniffed the air.

"He smells the blood," Joseph whispered. "Don't move, Naomi."

The wolf leapt on the stone overhang and spotted Leader, leaning against the tree.

Someone will die today.

Leader's vow hung in the air. The wolf crouched, ready to pounce.

"We cannot let this happen," Naomi said. She looked to Joseph, but Joseph was no longer at her side. He was now the panther. He lifted himself on his hind legs, swatted the air with his claws, and let fly a piercing scream.

Leader came to his senses. He saw the wolf crouched in front of him. He covered his face with his hands as the wolf leapt for his throat.

The wolf never reached him. The panther took two quick steps, caught the wolf in mid-air, and flung him to the ground.

The fight was over in a heartbeat. The panther sank his claws into the belly of the wolf. He locked his jaws around the wolf's head and lifted him off the ground, swinging him back and forth till the wolf was limp and lifeless. He dropped the dead wolf at the feet of Leader.

"Now," I said. "We have to go!"

"No," said Naomi. "He has to know who saved his life."

Following Naomi, we circled the tree. Leader sank to the ground. I came to life before him, and Nita joined me. Leader shook in fear.

"Who are you?" he said, trembling. We looked to the panther. Shiny black fur sank into his skin, his clothes appeared, and Joseph soon stood among us.

"You are the panther," Leader said. "That is how you survived that night in the cave."

"Yes," Joseph said. "I am the panther. And the boy you tried to kill."

"And you," he whispered, looking at Naomi. "I vowed that you would die today. Why did you save me?"

"It was the right thing to do," said Naomi. "It is the Choctaw way."

Leader looked hard at us. With the threat on his life gone, we saw his strength return. Leader kicked the wolf, and the carcass lifted from the ground. It fell at Naomi's feet, splattering blood in all directions.

Hearing the scuffle, the soldiers dashed to the river. They aimed their shotguns at Naomi and Joseph.

"One move and we will shoot you both," Roundman shouted.

"Put down your weapons," Leader said. "That is an order. We will return to our wagons now."

He turned to Naomi. "You have earned your life today," Leader said. "You can return to your parents. But there will be another day." For a moment that stretched into forever, we stood in silence and watched Leader walk away.

I felt a strong shiver and breathed a sigh of relief. Hundreds of Choctaw ghosts appeared, encircling us. A stout old Choctaw man stepped forward.

"I have heard of you young Choctaws," he said, casting a slow gaze at Joseph, Naomi, Nita, and myself. "I want you to know that I walk with you now."

"Who are you?" Naomi asked. "I think I have seen your face."

"I am Chief Pushmataha," the man said.

"My grandfather spoke of you," said Joseph. "You are General Pushmataha. You fought at the Battle of New Orleans."

"Yes," Pushmataha said, smiling. "I was a general in the United States Army. I come today to honor four young

Choctaw heroes. You are brave and you are honest. Young men, you rescued an innocent Choctaw. She will never forget how you risked your life to save her. Young lady, you saved a man's life today. You did the right thing."

We hung our heads, proud and embarrassed both.

"I hope you will never forget this day," Pushmataha continued. "Always remember, we Choctaws are a strong people, a good people. We fight to protect two nations, the United States of America and the Choctaw Nation."

"*Yakoke*," we said.

"*Yakoke* to you," Chief Pushmataha said, lifting his arms.

The gathered throng of Choctaws, a thousand strong, lifted their arms and whispered, "*Yakoke*," sending their thank you to the heavens. The trees rustled in the wake of a soft breeze.

Chapter 29

Pushmataha and the Choctaw Four

BY DAY'S END, the bonepickers had a new wagon and the burned blankets were replaced, as ordered by Leader. The soldiers delivered bags filled with ears of corn to every wagon of walkers. Naomi was reunited with her mother and father, and that very evening she insisted on helping with the cooking.

"Please," she said. "I can't sit still and be waited on."

"But this is your first day with your family," her mother said. "We are celebrating your return."

"Nothing will make me happier than to cook for my family, my bigger family," she said, looking at Luke and my mother and father.

"I want to help, too," said Joseph.

She and Joseph built a fire, fanning the sparks till yellow

and blue flames flickered and danced and warmed the air. Naomi and her mother, Ruth, boiled the corn to a thick broth, stirring the pot and smiling. Nita and I joined the gathering, in full view of everyone.

The Trail still lay before us. The winter was fierce and food was scarce, but our most feared enemy, Leader, left us alone to be with our families. We met a new friend and protector that day, as well.

We knew we would see General Pushmataha for many days and years to come.

"*Chi pisa lachike*," he told us, as he floated from our sight. "I will see you again."

Acknowledgments

I would like to acknowledge the following friends, research-ers, and encouragers for helping bring *How I Became a Ghost* to life: The many Choctaws who have generously shared their family stories for the past two decades will always be remem-bered. Gone-before Choctaws include Jay McAlvain, Buck Wade, Tony Byars, Archie Mingo, Lizzy Carney, and Estelline Tubby. *Yakoke* to language teachers LeRoy Sealy and Richard Adams, and to Stella Long, Tom Wheelus, and Helen Harris for their panther stories.

Thanks to Steve Hawkins of the Oklahoma Historical Soci-ety's research division, for guiding us to a good map of the vari-ous Choctaw Trails of Tear routes. I also want to acknowledge fellow members of the Choctaw Literary Revival. Inspired by Louis Owens, they include D.L. Birchfield, Roxy Gordon, Ron Querry, James Bluewolf, Phil Morgan, Lee Hester, Jim Barnes, LeAnne Howe, Clara Sue Kidwell, Rilla Askew, Donna Akers, John D. Berry, Devon A. Mihesuah, and Greg Rodgers.

I am forever indebted to Dr. Joe Moore for supporting my efforts to record tribal stories. Special thanks to museum advo-cates Susan Feller, Mary Robinson, and Mississippi Choctaw Martha Fergusen. *Yakoke* to friends and fire-lighters Charley Jones, Geary Hobson, Joe Bruchac, and Les Hannah.

About the Author

Tim Tingle is an Oklahoma Choctaw and an award-winning author and storyteller. His great-great-grandfather, John Carnes, walked the Trail of Tears in 1835. In 1993, Tingle retraced the Trail to Choctaw homelands in Mississippi and began recording stories of tribal elders. His first book, *Walking the Choctaw Road*, was the result, and in 2005, it was named Book of the Year in both Oklahoma and Alaska. He lives in Canyon Lake, Texas.

Discussion Questions

1. In *How I Became a Ghost*, there are many ghosts who make appearances throughout the story. Can you name three of them? Can you say whose experience inspired the name of the book?

2. What do Isaac and his family mean by "Treaty Talk"?

3. How did the older Choctaws say good-bye to their home?

4. What does *chi pisa lachike* mean? Why is this phrase so important to Choctaws? Why is it important to the story?

5. Why does Joseph hide from the soldiers? Now tell his escape story as if you were the panther.

6. Why does Naomi refuse to try and escape from the soldiers? What happens to change her mind?

7. Have you ever met a dog like Jumper? What makes him so special? Describe the Snow Monsters and how they came to be.

8. Would you like to spend a day with Isaac before he becomes a ghost, or after? Why?

9. If you were to be a ghost for a day, what would you spend it doing?

10. Who is Nita and what does Nita want more than anything?

11. What role do the Choctaw bonepickers have in Choctaw country?

12. When Naomi has a chance to leave the soldier who threatened to kill her to the mighty jaws of the wolf, why does she step in and save the soldier's life?

13. Have you ever forgiven someone who wronged you? If so, why?

14. Who is General Pushmataha, and why does he appear in our story?

North Canadian River

Arkansas River

Ft. Sr

CHOCTAW NATION

Choctaw Agency

Doaksville

Eagletown

Ft. Townson

Washingto

Sabine River

Trinity River

Choctaw Trail *of* Tears

Choctaw Nation, 1825-1855

Western Choctaw Nation, 1820-1825 (ceded by the Choctaws to the United States, January 20, 1825)

Ceded by Choctaws, 1820-1830

Removal route

Early settlement

U.S. Fort